INTRODUCTION AND DEDICATION

The story of Mansa Musa began as a historical pet project I started while I was writing my thesis. I dabbled in learning about the Mali Empire and the story of Musa's famous Hajj, in which he stopped in Cairo before reaching Mecca. The more I researched the more I became enthralled with the story of this Black Muslim ruler who ruled with an iron fist. As I got lost in maps, trade routes, prices of gold, and other aspects of this story I began to piece information together.

I tried my best to stick as close to history as possible. When reading this it is natural to wonder; what is true and what is false? Without giving away the story I will say: I stayed true to the line of succession. All of the kings or "Mansa(s)" are real people who lived real lives. The Hajj journey is real, although I shorted the time Musa stayed in Cairo. It is reported he spent three months in Cairo, but to not bore you I wrote of a three day stay.

Most importantly I want to stress this is a story about power and politics not culture and religion. I have no intimate knowledge on Mali or Malian culture which is why I did not focus too much on culture. I wish this book to be read as political suspense for that is the frame of mind I was in while writing it.

I have to give special love to the Muslims around the world, but especially all the Black Muslims. We have had our stories pushed aside for so long. In this I attempt to shed a glimmer of light on a forgotten story.

SOCIAL MEDIA

To help spread the word, please screen-shot or take a picture of the cover and post it on social media with the hashtag #MansaMusa. If you read a quote that you love please share it on social media with the hashtag #MansaMusa.

Feel free to follow me on social media-

Twitter: @amirMW

Instagram: @amir.webb

THE CATALAN MAP

Drawn in 1525, almost two hundred years after Musa's death; his image appears on a Catalan Map. He is depicted wearing a gold crown, holding a gold scepter, and holding a gold nugget. The story of Musa's wealth was well known in Europe and stood the test of time.

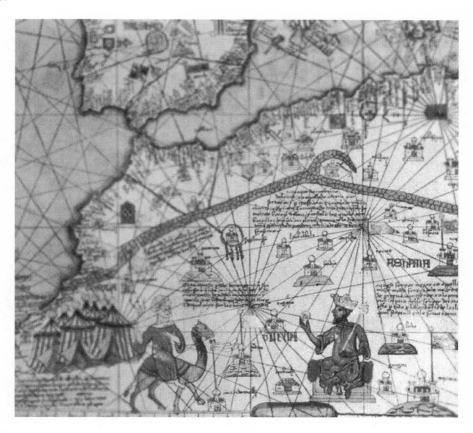

The Kingdom of Mema 1235

Sologon entered her son's hut without waiting for his call to enter. She finds him kneeling on his prayer mat finishing afternoon prayer. Whispering to Allah with his hands cupped, he wipes his hands over his face, completing his prayer. "The delegation is here to see you," she says while he kisses her on the forehead.

"After I told them not to come?" he asks. Deeply troubled at the prospect of the meeting he begins to pace back and forth in his hut.

Sologon places her hand over her son's hand, silently commanding him to be still. "Remember we are guests in this kingdom. We have been given royal status here because of our bloodline." He peaks his head out the entrance of his hut to see men on horse back, dressed in various fashions from the different kingdoms. "The days of running and hiding can be over. Hear what they have to say," she pleads as she forces him to make eye contact with her by taking his face between her hands.

"Send them in," he says reluctantly with a sigh. They enter, one by one, introducing themselves to him. The spokesman for the delegation introduces himself as Basil, but no introduction was needed. Basil knows him from the time he and his mother spent in exile in the Kingdom of Wagadou.

Basil embraces him as Sologon's son remembers the education Basil gave him. Arithmetic, Islamic studies, and anything else the young curious mind of Sundiata wanted to learn. "Sundiata, you have grown," Basil says pointing to his beard. The delegation from various kingdoms gather in a circle in the hut as Basil breaks the silence that has gripped them. "Your brother, Dankaran, has fled Niani, along with his mother." Sundiata is unmoved at the news, remembering that Dankaran exiled he and his mother. Sundiata, the rightful heir to his father's throne of Niani was pushed aside by Dankaran and his mother, Sassouma. Sent into exile, Sologon sought sanctuary, in the kingdoms of Wagadou and Mema where they currently reside.

It was in Wagadou where Sundiata was tutored by a young scholar named Basil. With the fear that Dankaran had changed his mind and sent men to kill them, Sologon fled Wagadou when Sundiata was fourteen. They were both welcomed in the Kingdom of Mema with open arms. Sundiata, although more legend than reality, was a popular name in the various kingdoms. People knew that, Maghan Fatta, had a son with his second wife, with the name of Sundiata, but that is all they knew. Some thought he was killed by Dankaran, some thought he had killed himself, damning himself to the hellfire. A select few thought of Sundiata as nothing more than a myth. But all the various kingdoms wanted to be saved from the oppression of the Kingdom of Kaniaga.

"By who?" Sundiata asks Basil.

"Harun, the King of Kaniaga. He has taken residence in Niani and is imposing a brutal occupation. None could be here from Niani today out of fear they would be followed by his men," Basil says.

"I am sorry brothers. I am unsure what any of this has to do with me," Sundiata says while giving them his best look of confusion.

"We are here, to ask you to unite the fractured kingdoms into one dominate empire. With you as ruler," Basil says as the delegates nod in agreement. Sundiata pretends to be in shock as he refuses over and over again, but they persuade him to take command of a united army. No persuasion was needed, Basil and Sundiata have been planning this meeting for a year. Sundiata's constant refusal to meet them and Basil's constant persistence that they meet, was all part of their plan hatched through letters. The delegates were desperate and Basil convinced them Sundiata was their only option, his refusal to meet only intensified their desire to have him lead them.

Barely eighteen, Sundiata marched a united force against Harun at the Battle of Kirana. After a year of fighting, Sundiata entered Niani for the first time since he was sent into exile as a child. People cheered and cried, as Sundiata, the exiled prince returned to free them of oppression. Harun slipped out of Niani in the cover of night, Sundiata took no great effort into finding him. It was Danarkan that he wanted.

He sent his men far and wide to find his half brother. When they found him, they dragged him before Sundiata. With the audience hall full of soldiers, Dankaran began to plead for his life. "Spare me brother! It was all my mother's doing!" he cried out. Sundiata, unmoved as always, looked down at Dankaran with disdain. From his throne, with armrests made of ivory, carved from ebony, and decorated with gold, Sundiata stood.

Sundiata placed his mouth next to Dankaran's ear and in a melodic whisper said, "I had to find you. No doubt, your mother had a role in all of this. Where is she?" Dankaran shakes his head rapidly signaling his ignorance of her location.

"Do you know where my mother is?" Sundiata asks sarcastically. Once again Dankaran shakes his head. Sundiata opens his hand as a solider passes him a spear. "In the palace, where she belongs," he says lifting Dankaran's chin with the tip of the spear. Tears of regret stream down Dankaran's face.

"Remember, we are brothers," Dankaran says. Sundiata takes the spear and drives it through Dankaran's chest.

Sundiata leans into Dankaran as he gasps for air, drowning in his own blood. "Half brothers," he whispers. Sundiata kicks Dankaran from his spear and throws it to the ground. As Dankaran lays on the ground, Sundiata walks towards his throne. He places his body against the gold and ebony throne, resting his arms on the ivory armrests. At the age of nineteen, after years in exile, the Battle of Kirina, and eliminating his half brother, an empire was born.

Sundiata of the Keita clan, established the Mandingo Empire of Mali.

MUSA AND SULAYMAN,

I am here in Taghaza meeting with the Al-Nasir of Egypt. We are negotiating a fair deal on the profits of Taghaza and the future of the salt mines.I want to avoid further conflict with the Egyptians here in the North. It seems as if we will settle on a fifty-fifty deal on all profits from the salt-mines, but nothing is finalized.

I want you two to remember there are many who wish to have you two as enemies, but you two are brothers first, and princes of the empire second. Your father would be proud at the men you both have become.

Delegates from the various clans from our great empire will be present for a Great Assembly Meeting.At this meeting many things will be discussed and voted on, including gold as an official currency for the empire, which has been controversial to say the least. I will also name Sulayman as official heir to the throne as I will leave him as deputy when I take my leave for Hajj. I hope this letter reaches you both in good health and blessings of Allah.

Mansa Abu Bakr II

Djenne, Mali 1310

I remember the first time my father took me to the palace with him. It was the day after my mother died from a high fever. He pulled me by my arm, hurrying my little legs to keep up with him. My father, a stablehand, put me to work that day. I remember brushing the hair of the horses in a certain way. I remember feeding them in a certain way. I remember calming them if they became afraid in a certain way. If I did not follow that certain way he would chastise me.

I remember that first day. It was also the first time I met Musa. He rode through the palace gate with his half brother and heir to the Mali Empire, Sulayman. Their Grandfather, Mansa of Mali, Abu Bakr II also rode with them. Sulayman and Abu Bakr handed their horses to my father, but Musa handed his horse to me. We were barely over the age of seven and worlds apart. He, from birth destined for great things, even if not the throne, he would never want for anything. As for myself, my life would be turned upside down. One day, while tending to the horses my father was trampled to death. The night my father died, I went back to the hut I once shared with my mother and father. I sat in the dark; hungry, alone and afraid. The townsfolk thought I was cursed and kept away from me, no adult would come to my aid or take me in. They said that I brought death to my parents. An evil spirit gripped my soul they said.

It was Musa, who came to my aid. He would sneak from the palace with food wrapped in cloth, scurrying his little feet to my hut. Musa even taught me how to read. By candle light, we would sit in my hut stuffing our face with rice and fish, laughing and reading. Sometimes we would sneak to the Bani River for a swim. That was our shared childhood.

In adulthood, Musa still brings me books and food, to the same hut. Unlike in our childhood, during the day I work as a fisherman while he works as a tax collector for his grandfather, Mansa Abu Bakr II. This is our shared adulthood.

"Bread and rice! Oh, and a letter from grandfather!" Musa shouts while I am sitting in my hut fixing a hole in my fishing net. He hands me the food wrapped in cloth and he enters my hut and sits down. Musa's fingers, not so little anymore, pass over the letters as he reads aloud careful to not miss a word. I fill my mouth with rice and hurry and chew to ask a question.

"Everyone knew he would choose Sulayman, this is not surprise right?" I ask trying to find some silver lining in him not being chosen. "Your time on the throne will come, and what a time that will be, right?" We both know that is highly unlikely, Musa technically is not in the succession. Next on the throne is Sulayman then Sulayman's son Qasa.

"I am the half brother and the one with no military experience. I know nothing, but taxes and books," he replies folding the letter and placing it in his pouch. I finish my food and look over at the book they he brought me. "Plus, tradition is tradition, Sulayman is next in line, but Grandfather loves theatrics. *The Lighting of the Darkness on the Merits of the Blacks and Ethiopians* by ibn al-Jawzi. I thought you might like it." Musa hands me the book and I thumb the pages.

"You are the smarter brother," I say trying to cheer him up.

"Have you gathered the courage to approach the love of your life?" he asks in jest.

"No changing the subject, this is serious Musa! When are the delegates going to arrive?"

"Some are already here and more arrive by the hour it seems," Musa says while peeking his head out of the hut then sitting back down.

"How was your journey into the hinterlands?" I ask.

"Long and draining, but all of the new taxes have been levied. Whenever I leave I miss Fajr and Magha. I was itching to come home. Can I ask you a question?" he says with a bit of uncertainty. It is as if he is afraid of what my answer will be. I nod my head. "Do you want to get married? Build a home? Have a family? Wealth? We are almost thirty," he murmurs as if he is trying to keep my failures a secret from some unknown and unseen judge. "People may start talking," he whispers. He and I are both aware that people in Djenne are talking. They have always talked, some blame me for the death of my parents. People avoided me in childhood and in adulthood, which is why my business suffers.

"Musa," I say while closing the book. "I have no money, or skill. I sell fish in the market. What more do you want from me?" I feel my face becoming warm with frustration. He puts his hands up and apologizes and says he never meant to offend me, simply asking as a friend. "I have been saving up to buy my own boat, when I have enough money, I will look towards a family. These situations, are easier on you. I have no family to help me with these things."

"Tell me if you need any help, Isa. I have always looked at you as more of a brother than Sulayman. I can offer more than books and rice."

"Musa, I love you like a brother, but I am truly fine. I can manage. I am on my way to the market right now, actually." Musa stands up and opens his arms for an embrace. He kisses me on the cheek and gives me salaams.

The rows in the mosque are straight as we stand shoulder to shoulder. The imam sings out Allahuakbar as we all, in unison, bow. It is dry and humid outside, but the mud brick walls of the masjid keeps us cool.

"Allahuakbar," I say while I lift my head from the floor. I turn my head to the right and then to the left, giving peace and blessings to the angels recording my deeds. As we stream out of the masjid after jummah, going back to our lives, people crowd around sellers of silk, meat, books, and other goods. I pass by a kola nut merchant who has baskets surrounding him under a tent shielding him and his merchandise from the sun.

Soldiers on horseback rush pass the market and make their way in the direction of the palace. Among them, Mansa Abu Bakr, draped in a purple robe. As I continue to my fish stall I see Aminta bint Dawud, her father is a very successful merchant. He ships goods as far as Ethiopia. Some say he has business ties that reach to Europe, at least, that is the rumor. She is admiring a pot being sold by an Arab merchant. They strike a deal and she hands him small bag of crushed gold.

Musa calls Aminta the "love of my life," although we have no history, unless you count the countless dreams I have had of her. I have dreams of praying fajr with her, eating meals together, walking to jummah together. Her skin, the perfect shade of black. Her hair, always wrapped in a piece of cloth that compliments her outfit. She has been confined to my dreams and conversation with Musa.

"Salaam-al-laykum," I hear from behind snapping me out of my daydream. Somehow I have made it back to my stand without realizing.

"Ah, Demba, wa-laykum-salaam, how are you?" I respond, clearing sweat from my forehead with my sleeve.

"All is well, thank you. How is business?" he says setting up his stand.

"Very well," although it is a lie it is a polite lie.

"Glad to hear it. I have goats if you're interested."

"Maybe, but not today," his conversation is starting to annoy me as it always does. He continues on about silk prices and news from the first day of the delegation meeting. Apparently the delegation decided not to make gold the standard currency. His ability with numbers will make him a great man one day, but today it makes him an annoying man. After Isha, exhausted and tired, I approach my hut with two men wearing military armor are waiting for me.

"Isa?" one of the soldiers asks. I respond with a nod. The other soldier hands me a white robe and tells me to put it on. He tells me that Musa wants me to attend the second delegation meeting. I do as I am instructed and ride with them back to the palace. The ride is short, but my heart is racing. When we enter the palace gates, a stable boy, no doubt a slave, runs up and takes the horses. This is the first time that I have been in the Great Hall and it is filled with delegates from all over the empire. The two soldiers escort me to an empty table in the back of the hall as they sit in silence.

The dim light of what seems to be hundreds of candles is enough for me to catch a glimpse of various faces, all different shades of black. The delegates at the table next to me are discussing how Sulayman should continue Abu Bakr's policy of limited military. At the table next to them, they are discussing how the deal with Al-Nasir will have to be replaced soon. The smell of burning incenses fills my nostrils as a plate of food and a cup is placed before me. The server bows and scurries off to his next task.

"Where is Musa?" I ask one of the soldiers. He sits in silence. I look at the other who sits in silence as well. The sound of drums fills the Great Hall as all the delegates stand. I rush to my feet not realizing what is happening. Everyone looks up at the balcony, which I did not notice until now. A figure appears as the drumming stops.

"Introducing, His Majesty, Mansa of Mali, Abu Bakr Keita II. Prince Sulayman Keita. And Prince Musa Keita." Rapid drumming shakes the hall again as Abu Bakr, Sulayman, and Musa step onto the balcony. Abu Bakr, slowly takes his seat on the throne made from gold, ebony and large elephant tusk armrests. The delegates bow as I rush to follow their lead with a clumsy bow.

"As-salaam-laykum," Abu Bakr says, straining his voice to reach the space in between the four walls of the hall. Everyone in the Great Hall responds in unison with wa-laykum-salaam. "Yesterday, much business was settled and once again I thank everyone for being here. Tonight, I want to introduce to you all my chosen successor and who will be deputy as I finally fulfill a pillar of our faith, hajj. Sulayman Keita, one day, Mansa Sulayman." Abu Bakr lifts Sulayman's arm presenting him to the hall. The Great Hall erupts in cheers as Sulayman stands up, waving to his soon to be subjects. A young man sitting close to the balcony, not so much older than myself, with a soft face and low beard stands up.

"Mansa Abu Bakr! Musa Abu Bakr!" he shouts the Great Hall slowly becomes silent.

"Who speaks?" Abu Bakr says as he scans the crown.

"Yusuf ibn Said. Your majesty."

"Ibn Said?" Abu Bakr says as Musa leans over and whispers in his ear. "Ibn Said? Yes, I remember. Your father was a great man, a fair judge. I wish I got to see him one last time before he died," he says in a regretful tone.

"Thank you your majesty. I hope to continue my father's legacy. But I do have a request." Abu Bakr nods his head giving Yusuf permission to speak. "Our great empire is still very young and although Sulayman would be a great leader, I and many others here wish to vote on the next Mansa." The Great Hall erupts with a mixture of boos, cheers, hisses, and fists banging on tables. Yusuf holds up his hand trying to hush the crowd's mixed reactions.

Sulayman and Abu Bakr pass whispers as Musa sits surveying the hall, we lock eyes and he gives me a sheepish smile. Abu Bakr raises his arm and the hall instantly goes silent. "This is highly unorthodox, you all do realize this?"

Ibn Said nods his head, as other delegates nod in unison as they pass whispers and ripped pieces of paper between themselves. "Your majesty to prevent tyranny from falling upon us, allow the empire to have a say in this matter which impacts all of us. The only unanimous agreement we can come to is the fact that we cannot agree unanimously. Your Majesty, open this to a vote." Cheers fill the hall as Abu Bakr looks between Musa and Sulayman. Abu Bakr sits with a look of deep concentration on his face for a few minutes.

"Each delegation will have one vote. You will write a name on a piece of paper," the hall once again erupts in another round of mixed reaction. Musa continues to sit calmly as slaves bring in paper, reed pens, ink, and a basket in the hall. As the delegates debate among themselves, one by one, they place a folded piece of paper into the basket. When all the votes are in, the bucket is brought to Abu Bakr who counts them while sitting on his throne leaving the entire hall in suspense.

Abu Bakr runs his wrinkled hand over his face wrinkled face. "With a vote of eight to four, Musa, is hereby named heir to the throne." Musa stands up as drummers pound away hailing the future Mansa of Mali. Sulayman's face turns to stone as the color drains for his face. He turns from his natural black to a sick gray. Like the color of the sky before a storm. Abu Bakr places his hand on Sulayman's shoulder, but Sulayman brushes him away and leaves the balcony in a rush. Musa comes down from the balcony and is met with bowing delegates reaching to kiss his hand. I stand up to leave the corner which I was placed, but the two soldiers stop me by placing their hands on my shoulders and pushing me to my seat.

After an hour, Musa and Yusuf are the only ones left as I sit in the corner. "Isa, come here, there is someone you need to meet," Musa says from across the hall motioning me over with his hand. Ibn Said and I exchange greetings, I tell him of my work as a fishermen and he tells me his story as a lawyers son.

"It would be irresponsible of me not to mention that Sulayman is still heir after you," Yusuf says as the pleasant conversation ends.

Musa pats both of us on the back. "Which is fine. We wanted me on the throne not a revolution. Sulayman will fall in line, I promise." Musa says with a reassuring smile. "Yusuf, you will be greatly involved in my administration, a top lawyer position," he says while nudging Yusuf playfully. "Do you mind giving us a few moments?" Musa says to Yusuf. Yusuf bows and we exchange salaams. We take a stairwell to the balcony overlooking the once crowded Great Hall. The room seems darker from the balcony, the floor below lit by candles is being cleaned by slaves.

"I want you as my Chief of Council, you will be my number two," Musa says bluntly. I turn around and find him sitting on the golden throne. I walk towards the balcony and lean over. I want make sure that I am not dreaming and that falling was a possibility.

Musa stands up and puts him arm over my shoulder and I place my arm around his waist, as we both stare gaze upon the empty hall. When we were children we would stand like this, hugging each other looking out on to the Bani River on those summer nights we snuck away. "My grandfather keeps non-Muslims in his administration. I want this to be an Islamic Administration top to bottom. What my subjects do and who they worship is up to them," Musa clicks his tongue at the idea of forcing people into Islam.

"Do you accept my offer? As my Chief of Council?" I hear a hint of desperation in his voice as if he actually believes he needs me. For years Musa has been the reason my belly was full. Now, he is asking me to help run his empire.

"I accept Musa, of course I accept." Musa relaxes back in his throne and looks over the hall, running his hand over the ivory arm rest. "Musa, I must confess I know very little on governing, you do know this right?"

"I am aware, do not worry about that. By the time I am crowned Mansa you will be well versed in all things administration," he says giving me a slight boost in confidence. "You, must be aware, that after today, life will never be the same, for either of us." The desperation in his voice has returned. The confident Musa that sheepishly smiled at me while he was sitting to the left of Abu Bakr faded away. The Musa in front of me, seemed unsure of his future, as if he knows history and the entire world is against him.

There was hope, that I would have time to educate myself on my future position, but one week after Abu Bakr returned from Hajj he died from a high fever. The same day of Abu Bakr's janaza, Musa became Mansa Musa, Ruler of Mali. During the coronation, drums rattled the ground of every part of empire, signaling the era of a new Mansa.

1313

Musa has made many changes in the short time that he has been Mansa. Those of us in his inner circle have been elevated beyond belief. Fajr, his wife and now Muso Mansa of the empire has taken to her role well. Their marriage was arranged well before Musa took the throne, more political than love some say.

Fajr is the sister of Umar, the king of the Gao Empire. They call him "The Night King," as the story goes, he had his brother, the former king, killed in the middle of the night and his body taken to the

17

desert and buried. There are others that believe Umar had his brother's body tossed in the Niger River. The story he tells is his brother could not take the pressures of the throne and left in the middle of the night on horseback, never to return. Either way, here, in Djenne, we call him Umar. He has a reputation for being ruthless with his foes and distrusting of his friends. Abu Bakr was looking for a suitable match for Musa and Umar presented his sister.

Their son, Magha, now a sophisticated teenager has taken up law and administration. Although Magha has gone through military training, it is obvious he has a mind for books and less for swords. Sulayman has been plucked from his role in the army and demoted to overseeing royal trade agreements along with his son Qasa who serves as Sulayman's aide. Musa elevated Sagaman, the son of a former military leader to the position of general of the military. Although Sulayman is still heir to the throne the dissatisfaction can be seen on his face, as if carved in wood, never changing. Sulayman thrived on his position in the military he has been a fish out of water ever since.

Timbuktu has been a point of interest, King Jarrah, a non-Muslim has been losing favor among his subjects and more importantly the scholars of Timbuktu seemed to detest him. Fajr has also been building soup kitchens for the poor, making her name known throughout the city. Within the year, doctors, lawyers, and artists have all seen generosity from Musa. King Jarrah us hanging on to power by a thread.

Then there is the gold. All gold in the kingdom is the property of Musa, as he declared all goldmines his personal property. Bambuk and Bouré, produce a majority of Musa's gold, as the land is worked by slaves and attracts merchants from trade routes all over, mostly Muslim traders. All gold is handed over to the royal treasury and is exchanged for equal weight in ground gold dust, with Musa taking a portion as tax. Gold dust and salt tablets are the common currency now, but gold and copper bars are still used in the rural areas.

Gold from the empire is sold to North Africa and even reaches across the waters to the Mediterranean. With this gold Musa was able to build an army that could crush any empire like an elephant crushes the grass under its feet. Most importantly, gold buys loyalty. I suggested to Musa that Demba, a man known for his great math ability, to head the royal treasury. Musa asked if I could trust him, and even though the thought of being in a room with Demba for longer than hour annoys me, he has always been careful with his words and his numbers.

With this influx of gold came the influx of slaves, a moral dilemma for myself, but a political necessity for Musa and the empire. The goldmines are largely worked by slaves, usually non Muslim men captured in Musa's quest for new territory in the interior of the empire. They are shipped to and from various goldmines in the empire and forced into labor. Never mistreated, as far as the Islamic laws governing slavery, nonetheless forced to do work and moved from their homes.

All of this, is done with the help of the man that stood up and demanded a vote at the delegation meeting, Yusuf ibn Said. He has emerged as Musa's legal advisor. The capturing of slaves needed to be justified legally, which was easy. The declaration of Musa owning all gold in the empire, needed a more complicated legal justification. Everything that Musa does needs a legal justification with roots in the Holy Qur'an. Yusuf, has a sharp mind and one day, he will reach the level of Ahmed Baba, our most famed scholor.

Musa and Sagaman through diplomacy and military action have expanded the tax base to include the Wolof and Fulbe people. The salt mines of Taghaza are still being shared fifty-fifty with Egypt, which was a deal that Al-Nasir and Abu Bakr reached before his death.

"Fifty-Fifty, no longer seems fair if my king's army is securing a majority of the trade routes to and from the salt mines," Al-Bari, the Egyptian ambassador relays the Egyptian king's uneasiness.

"When Al-Nasir came to power, again, we allowed him to place his army at the trade routes to secure his political power, and they never left. That's not our fault," I retort. Al-Bari strokes his beard as he motions for a slave to fill his cup with water. "Pull back your military, that is the only solution," I say. "Our tax collectors have been complaining that your military has been harassing them."

"You do not understand. We do not want to pull back our military, we want to adjust the agreement." The ambassador gulps down his water and places the cup on the map lying in front of us, covering Taghaza.

"Is that a threat?" I ask. The ambassador shakes his head and rises to his feet.

"Of course not brother. Fair is fair. Al-Nasir only wants what is fair and just. The original deal with Abu Bakr was not fair," he responds while leaning on the wall looking out the window gazing over Djenne. "Isa, we both know that was a place holder deal, so Al-Nasir and Abu Bakr could focus on domestic issues while winning a diplomatic victory. It is now time for the serious negotiations."

"Sir, Mansa Musa summons you," a messenger says through the door.

"Tell his majesty I am on my way," I reply. Musa summons me these days.

"Al-Bari," I say trying to gather my thoughts. "We will come to an agreement. Let me talk to Mansa Musa and we will finish this later," I say while gathering papers for my meeting with Musa. Al-Bari nods as I rush out of my office.

"Isa! Salaams," I hear a voice from behind me as I am rushing to Musa. I turn around and see Fajr and Magha, mother and son.

"Salaam, your majesties," I say while bowing deeply. "I have been meaning to catch up with you Magha, I hear excellent things about your law practice, Alhamdulillah."

Fajr looks at Magha like any proud mother looks at a child, this child just happens to be the son of the ruler of Mali. "All things are from Allah," he says as we all smile at his answer.

"And you Muso Mansa? I read a report of a number of food kitchens in Timbuktu you have supported?" I say while inching down the hall to signal my eagerness to leave. Fajr fixes her purple head wrap and intertwines her arm with Magha's.

"Nothing is more important to me than the making sure the people of this empire have all they need. Which is why there will be many more reports on your desk like that one. But, let us not keep you. Go, you have a meeting with Musa," Fajr says with a hand on my shoulder. I give my peace and blessings and scurry down the hall passing guards posted and slaves carrying fabric. It is hard not to notice she is speaking of Timbuktu as if it has submitted to Musa's rule.

I enter Musa's office without knocking as Musa is busy signing papers and giving commands to people buzzing around him like bees around a hive. The only people not moving are the twelve guards posted along the walls of the room armed with a spear in their hand a sword on their hip.

"Leave us!" Musa shouts and the room clears except for the guards who are a fixture to Musa's side.

"Salaam, your majesty" I say while bowing.

"It will never get old seeing you bow, but it is not needed in private. I have told you this Isa," Musa hugs me and we move over to a window overlooking the courtyard where military commanders are training military horses.

"How was the meeting with the ambassador?" Musa asks. I lay the papers on his desk including the map.

"They want to renegotiate the agreement, I am unsure what they actually want in all honesty," I reply.

"Have we heard from Ambassador Embrima about his counter talks in Egypt?" Musa asks. I shake my head no.

Musa sucks his teeth and moves back to his desk, "I need you to check in with the Head of the Treasury. Stress to him my eagerness to reestablish the communication system along the Niger. He has been dragging his feet on this matter, but we cannot have our tax collectors unable to reach us." Musa pauses, "As important as that is. There is another matter of importance. Remember Aminta?" Musa asks. Of course, but I lie and say no.

"I sent a letter of introduction to her family on your behalf, proposing marriage," he says with a sinister smirk. I look at him with my mouth open looking for words to say.

"Musa! Why would you do that!" I pause and try to calm myself by plucking dates from the bowl on the table and pouring some water. "What did she say?"

"Her father wants to meet you, of course! You are Chief of Council, who would not want you in their family?"

"So you think her family wants my status not me as a person?,"I say while chewing.

"All I am saying is that you are finally in a good position. Would you rather leave your position and test her love? Isa, meet her." I gulp down the last bit of water.

I stand up and pluck a few more dates from the bowl for the ride to the treasury. "Tomorrow," I say with a smile.

"Very well," Musa says clasping his hands behind his back. "You know, I think I will join you at the treasury. I need to get from behind these walls," he says.

The treasury is just as heavily guarded as the palace and just as large in terms of size. Some would argue that it is the most important building in Djenne, although some would claim the royal mosque is. The treasury is where a majority of Musa's gold, jewels, and ivory is held. The treasury is where people come to exchange their gold nuggets for crushed gold and where payment for government contracts are sent. As we approach the treasury, guards part the walkway leading to the main entrance. The highnoon sunlight splashes on the wagons of uncovered gold causing the illusion that the gold is illuminated from the inside. Slaves unload ivory as others examine the quality.

Musa and I, along with his miniature army that guards him pass through the gates of the treasury as everyone we pass bows. Demba greets us at the gate as walks around to inspect Musa's gold and jewels.

"Preparing for grain collection along the Niger, I see," I say pointing to the canoes being carved and smoothed out.

"Oh yes, the various villages along the river have been very productive. All have exceeded this years quota," he says while looking over a paper handed to him.

"But still, some will not submit to taxes," Musa says kissing his teeth.

We head inside while exchanging small talk. Inside the treasury, scribes are copying various treaties, receipts, and trade agreements. Sulayman, stands over a scribe, dictating words, no doubt a trade agreement that will soon be sent to Musa. "What do I owe this visit?" Demba says while we take seat at a table in the courtyard.

"The line of communication along the Niger, there is news it has come into trouble," Musa says. Demba nods his head in agreement.

"It is true, to an extent. The communication posts have been established. The issue is, these posts keep coming under attack by locals rebelling against your taxes." I sit in silence as Musa calls in a scribe.

"By what right do you have to rebel against my rule? Do any of you hold claim to the throne? Do I not protect you from invaders and thieves even though none of you are Muslim? Do you not trade freely with no interference? I, as Mansa, and you as subject have roles and duties, but let me be clear," Musa stops as the scribe, Demba, and myself look on. "Either I send canoes filled with tax collectors or canoes filled with soldiers. The choice is entirely yours. I pray by Allah you make the correct choice."

Musa instructs his brief speech be copied and sent to Segaman. "I want this read by Sulayman in every village that has rebelled." Demba takes a copy of the speech and hurries about his task. "I swear I will have each of these rebel's head on the end of a spear," he says, but not to me. He is looking away talking to himself.

I make my way to the house of Aminta bint Dawud. I know I can ride faster, but I take my time, enjoying the ride. Passing mud houses with balconies fixed on the side with women shouting from one house to another. Children playing, and soldiers rushing by heading back to the palace returning from some mission Musa sent them on. I clumsily dismount my horse and trip, getting dirt on my clothes. As I brush myself off the wooden door opens and two small children run out. "Be back before dark!" he says while approaching me.

The old man with no hair and a booming voice turns to me, "Salaam, Isa! We have been expecting you!" I gather myself and greet him with salaams and a kiss on each cheek. "Aminta is waiting for you in the library," he says while guiding me inside. "I have to ride into the market and pick up a few items, you two will be fine?" he asks. My hands are dripping with sweat and my mouth is as dry as The Sahara, but I nod my head as he takes his leave.

As I move into the library I see Aminta, on the floor, surrounded by books and papers. Her hair is wrapped in a red cloth. Her neck and arms exposed. I shake myself to reality and knock on the wall to announce my presence.

"As-Salaam-laykum, Aminta," I say with my eyes to the floor.

"Wa-laykum-salaam, I'm sorry you caught me while I was trying to reorganize this mess," she says while looking over the books.

"I can help," I say eagerly.

"Well, if you insist," she says picking up on my childlike eagerness.

25

"What are we doing," I ask.

"I had to look over my father's records for his business, there was a disagreement with a tax collector about some trading. I have been at it all week, but someone came by today and said the problem was resolved and they're sorry for the mistake. So now I have to it put all this back."

As we place books back in their proper place and make small talk, she turns to me while we are both kneeling on the floor, "I feel like I have seen you before, maybe in the market?"

I pick up a book, brush it off, and place it on the shelf. "I guess it is possible, certainly not impossible.

What were you doing, two years ago?" she asks inquisitively

"I was a fisherman."

"An actual fisherman?"

"Yes, I would catch fish then sell them. A fisherman."

"How did you..."

"Long story, very long story."

"We have time, tell me."

"Aminta, time for prayer!" a small voice yells from the door. Aminta slides the last book on the shelf and dusts herself off. The small voice was right, as soon as he leaves the ahdan echoes off of the mud brick buildings.

"My little brothers wait at the mosque for the muezzin to walk to the minaret. Then they run to as many houses as they can to tell people it is time for prayer before he calls it. They have made it a game among all the kids. Well, thank you for your help, I hope that I can hear on how you became Mansa Musa's Chief of Council soon."

"Of course, I should head back to the palace, I have meetings after salaah," I say while inching away from her. She looks at me with cautious eyes, as if I am hiding something, which I am. There is no meeting. My nerves are coming undone and I feel as though I must leave before I do or say something ridiculous.

"Well, then, off you go. Visit again soon," she says with a smile.

"Salaam-al-layum," I say while backing out of the room. On my way out I run into a table and break one of the legs while falling down. Aminta runs over to help me up, but all I can respond with is, "I can pay for that."

Musicians gather in a circle playing their drums and strings while people around them dance to the beat. Storytellers sit with children and their parents to tell the stories of the Qur'an and Mandinka stories. All of this is for the last day of our wedding festival. Aminta, dressed in a dark blue dress with her shoulders showing and her hair wrapped in a light blue cloth. Fajr and Aminta are in the dancing circle swaying their hips from side to side, not missing a beat. While walking around the various vendor stands, Musa and I, run into General Segaman.

"Salaam-al-laykum! And congratulations is also in order on your marriage!" Segaman says while embracing me. Since Musa promoted Segaman he has become a good friend, although much about him is still a mystery. He has the skill of being able to say a lot without saying anything of substance unless it is about war.

"Thank you, brother, I honestly thought she would say no."

"She still can," Musa says while laughing and nudging me with his elbow.

"Oh come now Musa, Isa is one of the good ones!" Segaman says.

"Prayer books and incenses!" a vendor yells. We make our way over to him and survey his merchandise.

"This may be a good one, 'Prayers of the Prophet,' how much?" Musa asks.

"A small bag of gold dust will get you five books, sir." Musa and Segaman look over the books while the sight of Aminta dancing catches my eye. Her hips catch every beat of the drum and her arms move to every pluck of the string. Her smile transfers to my face and I find myself smiling for no reason.

"Are you listening, Isa?" Musa asks. "What is so funny?" he asks, catching my smile.

"I heard you, paper merchant from Venice. I'll be there," I say rejoining the conversation.

"Yes, and Sulayman already made some kind of deal with him. Whatever is it I know Sulayman will allow him into the interior of the empire and set up his business," Musa says while sniffing an incense.

"We caught a few Christians from Europe stealing ivory a few weeks ago. We confiscated the ivory and sent them on their way. They were lucky we did not give them a blade to the neck," Segaman says.

"Exactly" Musa says pointing at Segaman. "They are trouble, especially when they think we are too busy to catch them. I will do business with him personally, Sulayman might not like that," Musa says shaking his head. "But it is what I must do for the good of the empire."

"He will be fine," I intrude. "He knows the rules in dealing with European Christians."

"Get him!" a little voice shouts and suddenly we are surrounded by a group of children pulling at our clothes and attacking us with small wooden sticks. The women stop dancing and look over at the spectacle of the three most powerful men in the Mali Empire overtaken by a group of children.

"Where are my guards!" Musa playfully cries out.

"There are too many of them!" Segaman says falling on the floor in laughter.

"Spare me! Spare me!" I shout running over to Aminta hiding behind her. "She's the one you want!" I yelp.

After Aminta and I prayed Isha, we head to our chamber in the palace. For the first time, we climb into bed to enjoy our first night as husband and wife. She lays her head on my chest. "What else do you want?"

"What do you mean?" I respond.

"Do you only want to be Chief of Council?"

"I never really thought about it. The next best thing would to be king," I say jokingly.

"One thing I have noticed is that Musa is the sun and all good fortune comes from him in this kingdom. If for whatever reason you loose favor with him..."

"What are you saying?" I interrupt,

"Nothing," she says. "Nothing." She kisses my lips and strokes my bead until we both fall asleep.

The next morning, commotion outside the palace wakes me before the fajr adhan is called. I get dressed and go outside to a caravan of wagons being brought into the palace gates. I loose count at thirty-five wagons, but no doubt all of these wagons are filled with Musa's gold. I look closer and realize some of the wagons are carrying people. I approach one of the wagons and two guards on horse back follow me as I walk the length of the caravan.

"Let me see the what is in the wagon," I demand. The man does what he is told and removes the cover from the top of the wagon uncovering gold nuggets. I cover them back up and move to the next wagon.

"This one," I say while pointing, but I already hear the cries of the people in the back. When the back of the wagon is opened, I see black bodies huddled together in fear. I hide my disgust and have the back of the wagon covered. The fajr adhan is called as I faintly here it from the tail end of the caravan. I motion the caravan to keep moving inside. Wagons seem to be emerging from the bottom of the sun as they keep pouring inside.

"Where is this paper merchant?" Musa asks Sulayman as we wait on the balcony of the audience hall. Musa shifts in his golden throne as Sulayman and I stand next to him.

"Stay calm brother he will be here. I am sure he got caught up in other business," Sulayman replies.

Musa looks over at Sulayman and his eyes narrow with impatience. "What other business is there in Mali if not with the Mansa of Mali?" Musa's voice was loud enough that even the people below doing business stop and look up at us. I shift my weight nervously from one foot to the other. I feel a hand on my shoulder and turn around to see Magha draped in a white robe.

"Salaam everyone, I am sorry for my absence from the festival yesterday. My journey from Timbuktu ran late. But, father safe to say all is well with our plans," Magha says. I am not sure when Magha became a diplomat or the plans he speaks of, but it is good to see him.

"That makes me glad, you did good son," Musa replies with a smile.

"Uncle," Magha bows to the Sulayman.

"Nephew," Sulayman refuses eye contact with Magha, but slightly bends his neck.

"Here he is," Sulayman says like a proud father showing off his son.

"From the city of Venice, Gyan..Gryaan..Giran?" the herald stumbles over the foreign name.

"Giradino de Parma, your majesty. Book and paper merchant," he bows and the court goes silent. Girandino, in his leather riding boots and long sleeved white shirt bows to Musa. His face is red and pink and his hair, a stringy mess as if he raced a horse to get here instead of riding one.

Without looking at any of us, Musa whispers, "he is so... pink."

"I hear you want to sell your merchandise in my kingdom? Prince Sulayman has said many good things about you," Musa says loudly from his throne. Whenever Musa calls Sulayman, "Prince," Sulayman instinctively smiles at thought of one day being Mansa.

"Yes, your Majesty, Prince Sulayman and I have made a deal the only thing it needs is your royal blessing" Giradino says. Musa stands and looks over the audience chamber filled with merchants, diplomats, slaves, military men, and regular citizens.

"I have looked over your contract that you and Sulayman reached. I decline," Musa says. Sulayman bites his bottom lip as I look at him out of the corner of my eye. "You will be allowed to sell paper, but only to me. I will be your one and only client. I can have no Christians dealing business in the empire on such a scale in which the contract demanded."

Girando looks around the hall for an answer and approaches the balcony when four archers take aim at him. The sound of unsheathing swords fills the audience hall. Musa raises his arm and allows him to approach. Girando gets on one knee, "I am thankful for your royal business. I look to serve you with the best paper for your royal usage."

"Tonight we will have a feast in honor of our new," Musa stalls looking for the right word, "union." Giradino bows his head and his yellow hair falls into his face. Sulayman leans into Musa's ear and whispers something and Musa replies with a pat on Sulayman's chest and whispers something back. Sulayman's face almost becomes unrecognizable when his eyebrows are pointed inwards in frustration. Just like the night he sat beside Abu Bakr and was denied the throne. Magha and I take a seat as subjects enter and Musa passes judgments from the balcony. Musa buries his face in his hand, "one more, it is almost time for Asr," Musa tells one of the court servants.

The court herald introduces a husband and wife; along with their lawyers. The wife is seeking a divorce on the grounds of domestic violence and infidelity. As the two parties are being introduced, Fajr enters the balcony and takes her seat next to Musa as Magha and I stand up and greet her. Musa and Fajr share a kiss and Musa waves for the lawyers to make their claims.

"So there is no evidence that he ever hit her?" Musa says to the wife's lawyer.

"No, your majesty, only client testimony, in these cases the evidence is physical and usually heals before the ruling," he says. Musa looks back at Magha and waves him forward. They share a few whispers and Magha takes his seat. Fajr opens her mouth, but Musa puts up a finger to silence her. "Let me think this over and I will send a verdict but, for now, she must return to her husbands household." Fajr looks at Musa with a glaring stare and she stands up with grace and leaves the balcony without words.

"Council meeting tomorrow after duhr. Make sure you're on time," Musa tells us and takes his leave.

As the feast in honor of Girando comes to a close, I notice that I have not seen Sulayman. His wife Aza and son Qasa, are present mixing and mingling. Musa and Fajr sit on their thrones on the elevated platform of the dining hall. They speak to each guest one by one, as they leave. Musa and Fajr, share a brief chat with Yusuf ibn Said and his wife. Aminta and I, after talking to Demba and his wife, exchange farewells as they leave. After a while, Musa, Fajr, Aminta, and I are the only ones left in the hall. Fajr and Musa, still sitting on their thrones, motion us over. "May I steal this lovely wife of yours?" Fajr asks.

Fajr and Aminta, lock arms and exit the hall. Musa motions me to sit next to him in the empty dining hall. After sharing a few laughs and discussing topics for the meeting tommorw, we go our separate ways. As I head back to my chamber on the opposite side of the palace, Girandino waves me down from the courtyard where he was passing through.

"What a great feast! The food is not what I normally eat and it was a little spicy, but I did enjoy it," he says patting my shoulder. "Tell me, what is new in the kingdom of Mansa Musa," he whispers.

"New? Musa builds new schools and libraries all over the kingdom," I say with pride.

"Right," Girandino says with a hand on his hip, "schools." I nod my head in agreement. "Nothing else?" he asks. I remind him that Musa values education above all.

"You know Isa, the only thing more valuable than gold is information," he says.

"I'm glad we are in agreement on the importance of education," I respond with a smile. Girandino returns my smile and leaves the courtyard with a confused look. I take a seat on a bench in the courtyard and gaze up at the night sky. I have never seen the courtyard so empty before. During the day, the courtyard is a hub of activity. Two men, enter the courtyard with a cart covered with a thick blanket, escorted by two young men holding torches. A large table is brought out and large pieces of paper.

The two men look up at the stars and point, while they trace something on the paper. Full of curiosity, I walk over and ask what they are doing. They seem to have not heard me so I stand there waiting for either of them to see me. As they look back up in the night sky, I touch one of the papers on the table.

"Be careful," one man says while still gazing up at the sky.

"What is it?" I ask again.

"Knowledge of the Moment of the Stars and What in Portends in Every Year" he replies, "Mansa Musa commissioned us to study the movement of the stars."

"Is it going to be a book?"

"Insha'Allah," one man replies.

I realize I may be more of am annoyance than a curious specter so I head back to the bench, gazing up at the stars, trying to see what the men see.

"Direct talks talk with your Majesty and Al-Nasir would be much more effective than myself speaking through the ambassador," I say with the entire council gathered.

"And still nothing from Ambassador Embrima in Egypt?" Musa asks while looking over a map of the empire.

"No, your majesty, we have sent many letters and still no response. Al-Nasir has sent no response either on his possible whereabouts," I reply.

Musa takes a dagger from his hip and playfully tries to balance the tip on the table. "We have a missing ambassador," he says, placing the dagger back on his hip. "General, what is the state of our military? I also need an update on securing trade routes. We can't allow all our trade routes to fall apart," Musa looks at me with a side eye as he asks Segaman for the update of the military in the interior.

"We have the trade routes secure and tax collectors posted. Magha was essential in establishing the tax posts. All will be well, your Majesty," Sagaman says with an air of confidence. Musa goes down the table and gets updates one by one from various counselors. "Sulayman, is the new deal with your paper merchant finalized? Such a shame to have a feast and no contract," Musa says.

"All that is needed is your signature," Sulayman hands the paper to a slave who walks it over to Musa. Musa takes the paper from the slave, but does not look away from Sulayman. The two brothers are locked in a staring contest in front of the entire council. Sulayman breaks the silence, "Your Majesty," he says reluctantly.

Demba gives Musa an update on the treasury, telling him that Bourè is safe and secure. Yusuf goes over the legality of a tribal war within the kingdom. Yusuf reminds Musa that it is his job to forge peace among the tribes, stating that it would be useful to use the Quranic reasoning to send a message of peace and brotherhood.

"Very well, keep me updated on the trade routes. As-salaam-alaykum," Musa rushes out the door going to his next meeting when Sulayman locks eyes with me.

"Isa, can we speak for a moment? I want to go over some of these figures with you," Sulayman asks as the room grows empty.

"Which figures are in question," I ask while shuffling through papers.

"I am the heir to the throne, you know this, right? One day I will occupy the seat in which my brother fills. Then my son, Qasa will sit on the throne, not Magha." I stop looking through the papers and realize he does not have any figures in mind. "Although I am heir, I find myself the most isolated person in the council, why is that?"

I fold my arms and lean back in the chair, "I can talk to Musa for you. Include you in more projects?" Sulayman gives me a look of curiosity then lets out a sarcastic laugh.

"You talk to Musa? I think, Isa, that is the problem. You talk to Musa. I think you're more ambitious than you allow people to believe. Am I right?" Sulayman moves towards me and stands behind me as I stare straight ahead. I do not have the courage to turn around.

"I have seen what happens to men without ambition, but would I call myself ambitious? No," I say without turning around.

"Like your father? No ambition? Died a stableman, right? And your mother died in childbirth, you never knew her?"

"Correct," I reply with a straight neck still facing forward. I begin to gather my papers when Sulayman wraps his hands around my neck. The papers fall and I being clawing at his face like a rodent battling a snake when being coiled. Like the rodent my counterattack is worthless as I move about in the chair grasping for air accepting my fate.

"Remember, Chief of Council, you came from a very low place and rose very quickly. The higher one climbs the deadlier the fall is. I hope you remember this when you speak with Musa." There is a certain venom in Sulayman's words. He releases me and walks out of the room leaving me to catch my breath in a pool of my own tears.

Now that I am Chief Council I can do something that I wished to do a few years ago; walk into the library and read. Although I spend a lot of time in the palace and on the palace grounds, I escape to the library, a short ride away. Surrounded by merchant stands and mud brick dwellings and stores, the masjid and library share the same space. In fact, many buildings act as mosques on top of their original purpose. Lawyers, scholars, patrons enter in and out daily seeking advice and materials. I hand my horse to a stable boy and he scurries off with my horse. I walk by the merchants and walked up the steps to the library for a day away from the hustle and bustle of court life.

I enter the shadowy main hall as students sit practicing Arabic on wooden boards. The heavy smell of incenses fills my nose as I inch by the lawyers and clients going over pending cases. Liberians and scribes slide by me as I make my way to the upstairs library when I spot Magha on a ladder reaching for a book with a young boy holding the ladder steady. Magha drops the book on the floor as another young boy picks it up and runs it to its proper destination.

"Working hard I see?" I say jokingly as he carefully climbs down the ladder to embrace me.

"Working hard indeed, on filling the shelves of the new library in Timbuktu my father is having built," he responds in almost an annoying voice.

"New library? Did I miss the plans for this?" I ask with an air of eagerness.

"No, no, this is supposed to be a secret so this stays between us." Magha moves me into a hallway away from prying ears. "I was in Timbuktu to bring an update back on the construction of the library. Now that father has secured paper, he can buy it then give it away. Uncle Sulayman was going to buy paper then sale it, potentially creating a monopoly," Magha leans against the wall and looks down as old men carrying a hand full of books shuffle by.

"What does the king of Timbuktu have to say about this?" I whisper.

"He has become more of a figure head now. Father has secured the trading routes and popular support in Timbuktu. In my opinion..." Magha checks the hallway for anyone. "Father will take Timbuktu and more than likely without bloodshed." I have been in the dark on this entire scheme, Sulayman's anger now makes sense.

"Magha, what do you know about the situation in Egypt?"

"Not much, father only has me working in Timbuktu, why what happened?"

"Nothing, I was just wondering, I have to pick up some books from upstairs, I am sure we will speak again soon." We exchange salaams and I make my way upstairs to a room occupied by Ahmed Baba, one of the oldest and most respected scholars in Djenne. They say he has lost a tooth for every one hundred books he has read; he only has four teeth left. There has been many times where I enter Musa's office without knocking, but when I visit Ahmed Baba, I knock and wait to be called inside.

"Yes, yes, Isa, come in, come in," Abu Baba responds.

"As-Salaam-laykum Ahmed Baba, you look well" I say. Ahmed Baba in his old age moves with grace as he stands up from behind his desk and moves over to share an embrace with me.

Wa-laykum-salaam, Isa, I see Musa let you roam with the common people today," he says playfully as we sit next to each each other.

"I sent a letter to you telling you I was coming today. I even attached a list of books I wanted to borrow."

Ahmed Baba laughs and shakes his head. "Paper is the one thing that I cannot keep up with," he points to the mountain of papers decorating his desk and the piles of books spread across his office. "What were you hoping to find?" he asks.

"There was a philosopher, Al-Amiri, he was of the Aristotle school of thought."

Ahmed Baba cuts me off. "Yes, the one who wrote that the master has a natural superiority to the slave, like a husband is natural superior to the wife. Why on earth would you want to read him and all his nonsense?"

"I was thinking of buying a few slaves," I respond.

"The natural state of every human is freedom, now, The Qur'an does not abolish slavery, but it is my opinion that we can move past such institutions. Let me remind you your wife is not your property. Don't read those books, it messes with your thinking," Ahmed Baba waves his hand in the air and declines my request for the book.

"I feel unprepared for this life" I confess. "I was a fisherman and before that a simple son of a stableman. Now I am Chief Council to the king of Mali? I am not cut for this work. Maybe buying a slave will make people at court respect me more." I stand from my seat to shield my tears from Abu Baba, but I know he heard them in the cracking of my voice. I burry my face in the open window facing the busy market.

"You know," I hear from behind me, in that familiar raspy voice, "there was a freed slave, Sakura, who became king of Mali. He took the throne from Abu Bakr, the first one obviously. He was eventually killed on his way home from Hajj. More than likely by an army officer."

I turn to him with a look of confusion. "Is any of that supposed to make me feel better?" I snap.

"You're not the first person to find themselves in this...uncomfortable position, but you have two choices. The palace or back to your old life."

Ahmed Baba is right. I only have to options and they are polar opposite of each other. Either I make this work or it is back to the hut and this time I may not have Musa to help me. I embrace Ahmed Baba and ride back to the palace. When I hand my horse to the stable hand a servant hands a note to be which says Aminta and I are to meet Musa and Fajr for a meal after Maghrib.

As Musa, Fajr, and Aminta, and myself are talking and enjoying our rice and fish I notice there are no guards posted in the room. Although I am certain that they are posted outside it feels nice that it is just us, even if moment is brief.

"We do have a request, more like a suggestion," Aminta says.

Musa looks at me and rolls his eyes. "Here here I thought you two just wanted to have a nice meal, but there is a catch," he says. Fajr runs her long black finger around the rim of her cup.

"I know you're going to be taking over Timbuktu soon," she finally says after taking long gulps of her water.

"We also know about the library," Aminta adds. It seems I was the only one who was left out of these plans.

"So... what is your suggestion?" Musa asks.

"Fajr and I want to open a school for girls only, so learn sharia and especially as it pertains to issues that impact women the most, like divorce."

Musa turns to me. "You knew of this?"

"Please Musa, I was clueless on Timbuktu and the school," I reply sinking back in my chair pretending to be devastated.

"I was going to tell you, I promise" Musa says, but I wave him off directing my attention back at our wives.

"Women need to have their own agency, educated on their rights and the such", I can hear the passion in Fajr's voice. Aminta silently nods in agreement with every word of Fajr's.

"The way you sent that woman away, the one who came to you looking for a divorce from her abusive husband? Remember?", Fajr asks and Musa replies with a slow nod. "She is going to go back to her parent's house and end up back with her abusive husband based on some legal opinion by a local judge", Aminta says with just as much passion drips in every word that leaves her mouth.

"So you think women will come to some different judgment," Musa asks.

"I think a woman who knows her rights can better defend herself in court instead of being at the mercy of men who can't sympathize with her," Fajr says as Aminta nods in agreement.

"So wait, women lawyers trained in Timbuktu is what you want?" I say plainly.

In unison they both say yes.

Musa runs his hands over his bald head and strokes his beard in defeat. He is about to speak when there is a knock at the door. "Yes! Please enter," but what he really meant was save me from this conversation. A messenger walks into the room and hands Musa a letter. Musa reads the letter and his eyebrows turn inwards.

"Where is the Egyptian Ambassador!" Musa's voice has the force of thunder. He doesn't ask anyone in particular, but he asks the entire room.

I decide to be the spokesman for the room, out of all of us I am the one that should know, "I will find him, your Majesty."

"Find him and bring him to me in the audience hall," Musa shoves the letter into my chest knocking me off balance. I look it over and my eyebrows raise in disbelief.

"What is it!" Fajr asks.

"We lost the salt mines in Taghaza."

MUSA,

I hope this letter finds you in good health. As your Northern brother I wish nothing more than peace between our two empires. Your grandfather and I sat down as brothers in faith and agreed upon a fifty-fifty deal after much debating. The goal was to once and for all end any armed conflict between our two empires. In my own empire I have had many setbacks and now I am on my third reign as Sultan. I am surrounded by enemies and I hope in you I have a friend.

This is why, I must say, the slave revolt against your tax collectors in Taghaza was not of my doing. I would never betray the words I spoke to your grandfather. The murder of your tax collectors was a sin against Allah. Do know, I have your ambassador under great protection and he is under around the clock guard, in case his life be in danger. I hope this issue can be resolved soon as I sent my own military to protect the salt mines from any further crimes.

Your brother in faith,

Al-Nasir Mohamed

I try to return to talk to Musa after delivering a sealed note to Al-Bari and General Segaman, but when I try to enter the chamber a guard blocks the door. I am told Musa is not seeing anyone, an emphasis on anyone. That was hint for especially me. The audience hall is buzzing with merchants making deals, lawyers listening to clients, and politicians politicking, and me waiting. News of the salt mines has not yet reached the public.

Al-Bari walks into the room escorted by twelve soldiers in full military gear, something is happening. My heart drops into my stomach. The drummers in the hall make Musa's entrance known throughout the palace. Musa walks on to the balcony with more

44

jewels on than I have ever seen on a person in my entire life. Two heavy gold chains hang from his neck, ruby, emerald, and sapphire rings hug his fingers. He is wearing all white and has his head wrapped in the typical style when one rides to cover their face from sand during a journey. With every thud from the drums, courtiers and slaves alike enter the hall. All pausing and looking up at the spectacle of Mansa Musa.

"Do you know the history of my tribe?" Musa asks Al-Bari. This was not the same confident and self assured Al-Bari I talked to a few weeks ago. Al-Bari searches his mind for an answer and looks up at Musa.

"You do not have the right to look at me! Keep your eyes down!" Al-Bari quickly lowers his head.

"I am unaware of the history, your majesty," he says while trembling in fear.

Musa takes a seat on his throne as he taps his palm on the tip of the elephant tusk armrest. He kisses his teeth and takes a deep breath. "It is said that Bilal had twelve sons, one of whom established the Keita tribe, I can trace my lineage to a Companion of the Prophet. Do you believe this story?" Musa asks.

"I could not think of a more noble story for a more noble tribe, your majesty," Al-Bari's eyes still fixated on the ground.

"You don't believe me or my story. You're saying that only because with the wave of my hand I can have your head parted from your body." Musa raises his hand and two soldiers place Al-Bari on his knees and bend his head, exposing the back of his neck. Another soldier takes out his sword. Al-Bari lets out a scream that I have never heard come out of the mouth of a human.

"Tell me why I shouldn't kill you!" Musa roars. Al-Bari, sniffling and crying cannot find the words to beg for his life. "Return to Egypt, tell your king, Al-Nasr, his greed will be his undoing." Musa vanishes from the balcony and the soldiers leave Al-Bari in a pool of his tears, grasping for air, in the middle of the audience hall.

I dodge groups of soldiers rushing to their destination in the hallway. I turn a corner and see Magha in military gear surrounded by lower level army officers.

"Prince Magha," I say formally and direct. "May I have a moment?" Magha looks at me and adjusts the sword hanging from his hip. The sword seems too heavy for his body and awkwardly placed.

"I will meet you in the quarters, leave us," he tells the officers. He turns to me and wraps his hand around my upper arm, basically pulling me. "You need to talk to father. He is questioning how you could let this happen."

"Me? I was only giving Musa the information that I was given." I realize I am yelling and quickly lower my voice in the crowded hallway. "Where is he?"

"In with Uncle Segaman and other high officers. Uncle Sulayman, suggested to father I get my first taste of battle." I can hear the false confidence in his voice.

"Musa is going to war with Egypt? He is leaving Sulayman as Deputy?" I ask nervously.

"He is the next in line for the throne, that is his right. That is how things are always done, it is tradition," Magha says gripping the handle of his sword. Still speaking with a false sense of confidence.

After a staring contests with the guards they move and allow me to enter. As soon as I enter I knew I made a mistake. Sulayman and Segaman among others are huddled over maps and papers.

"Salaam-al-laykum Mansa Musa," I say while bowing. Musa walks over to me and with an open hand slaps me to the ground. I gather myself as everyone in the room watches me stand up.

"This is your doing! I gave you one task! You have not only failed me, but you have failed this empire!" Musa slaps the other side of my face with the back of his hand. I keep my composure and allow Musa to discipline me the way he sees fit.

"We will talk about your future when I return. Until then stay out of the way of government dealings, do I make myself clear?"

Fighting back tears I bow my head, "Yes, Mansa Musa."

Musa looks me in my eyes and we hold eye contact. Not the eye contact of equals, but of sovereign and subject. The type of eye contact that is forbidden. As I begin to leave, Musa motions for the guards to block the door. Still fighting back tears, Musa takes one hand and places it around my neck, slowly tightening his grip around my throat. He pulls me close to him and whispers in my ear, "I made a mistake trusting someone just above a slave with matters of kings." He lets me go and motions for me to leave.

"In fact," his he says as I halt my movement. "You are relieved of your duties, stay at your wife's house." I bow my head, but not before catching a glimpse of the faces around the room. Segaman with his face full of disappointment, opens his mouth to speak, but decides against it. Sulayman with his back straight and eyes firmly planted on me knows that he has won. He has won without me knowing that we were at war.

War drums signal to the entire community that Mansa Musa will lead his army against the enemies of the empire, this time Egypt. Musa, dressed in thick military quilt armor, which protects against arrows and swords alike, rides the length of the rows of soldiers. Segaman and Magha ride behind him. When they reach the front, the one thousand man army marches behind them, slowly leaving the city gates.

Hundreds of his subject's cheer and clap as the army marches towards an uncertain future. As I look out of the window of Aminta's house, I catch a glimpse of the spectacle. She sneaks behind me and wraps her arms around my waist and kisses the back of my ear.

"I'm sorry," I whisper to her. "I have failed you. I have failed us."

ISA,

On our way to Taghaza the army was attacked by an unknown group. They were not looking to destroy us. Their numbers were too small. We came under the attack of skilled archers. Musa was hit with an arrow in the arm and chest. Magha hit in the leg. Both of their injuries at this very moment are critical. As I write this we are returning home. I hope this letter finds you in time.

- General Segaman

A week after Musa marched the army towards Tagazha, Djenne returned to normal, but my life has not. I am unsure if my life ever will be "normal." I have been ousted from my position in the council. We have been staying at Aminta's family home since leaving the palace. With the little gold I have saved I have started construction on a house of our own. Being removed from my position, Aminta and I have relied on her income from her father's business. My mornings are no longer filled with meetings with dignitaries and government officials, but with children playing and Aminta cooking, a regression to her former life.

I want to ask Aminta if she is happy, happy in her previous life, which now includes the burden of my presence. The truth may be a bitter one to swallow, but she could easily lie and tell me her heart is content. I wonder if she became accustomed to the slaves attending our every need, talking to Fajr while eating, living the life I always envisioned we would have and more. I asked Musa once, if he believed that her family was only interested in me for what I was, that seems like a silly question in retrospect. Who I was, was a person that Musa built and could destroy like rain destroys an ant colony.

Dawud, Aminta's father, asks me to accompany him into the market some days to help with the shipments coming in from the interior of the empire, usually ivory. These trips into the market have become bonding session between us, where we ask each other questions. I ask him why he never remarried after his second wife died giving birth to his twin boys. On one trip he was curious as to how Musa and I came to meet, given my background of poverty and his of everlasting wealth. We exchange answers, share laughs, sometimes we share tears, but we always share the truth.

Two weeks have gone by, and still no news from the army. The markets still buzz and the adhan is still called from the many minarets in Dejenne. After jummah, Aminta's younger brothers dig holes in the dirt collect and small rocks and beg me to play mancala with them. As we sit in the dirt playing, Dawaud is in front of the house reading, looking up whenever one of them accuses me of hiding pebbles in my sleeves. In the middle of our game a soldier in full military attire rides towards us at full speed stopping inches away from the children. They jump up in fright, but then stare in amazement as the soldier dismounts. I direct them towards their father. The soldier hands me a folded piece of paper from his pouch, I read over the note once, then twice, my knees buckle under the thought of living under the rule of Sulayman, even though I was no longer in the government. There was no way he is going to let me live in peace. The soldier tells me another messenger is behind him, he assumes he is carrying the same message , but for Sulayman. What does Sagaman expect me to do with this information? He was in the room when Musa slapped and banished me from the palace. He stood there, wanting to speak, either for me or against me, but too afraid to do either.

I tell the soldier that I need his horse as I move as race to the library to see if Ahmed Baba for consultation. I burst in the library dripping in sweat moving as fast I can to Ahmed Baba's office without looking suspicious. When I enter I tell him the contents of the letter:

Musa and Magha, father and son, have both been injured and for all we know, dead. He tells me there is nothing we can do, but wait for confirmation of Musa's death or survival, but what is certain is that Sulayman has suddenly been fitted with a new type of power, the power of political uncertainty. Much can happen when one has the power of uncertainty on their side because everything they say may be true.

I have the letter from Segaman copied and sent to Fajr, giving her a heads start if she wishes to flee before Sulayman's furry is released on Djenne. After a week, Sulayman closes the gates of Djenne. He believes the plotters of the attack on his family have come from inside and may still be here. Prices for everything begin to increase, movement has been restricted in and out of the city. The treasury, the second most guarded place in the city, has increased in activity. At first I assumed that Demba was a busy man per usual, trying to see what he could do to fix the economic crisis, but he was not in the treasury, he was waiting for execution. The news spread like a bush fire, Demba was guilty of treason, conspiring to kill Mansa Musa and Prince Magha. Although no evidence was presented against him, someone had to be blamed, and the people called for justice.

Demba was taken into the public space, in front of the people of Djenne. The women, children, men, ambassadors, foreign merchants, his family, gazed on as he was put to death. One blow from the sword of the executioner and Demba's head was removed from his body. Nobody clapped or cheered, only prayed that Allah would forgive the executioner for doing his duty. There are no prayers for the convicted. Demba, known for his purposeful thoroughness was no more, innocent or not, Sulayman had convinced the public that he was guilty. Demba had been jealous of Musa, spent years admiring Musa's gold, and plotted to steal it. Demba killed Musa and was planning to kill Sulayman next , but Demba was caught before he enacted the coupe to kill Sulayman and crown himself king.

As I try to maneuver my way around the crowd two soldiers grab me and tell me to follow them. I dare not resist and follow them into the palace were Qasa, Sulayman's son is waiting for me. Qasa is seated on a large pillow plucking dates from a bowl. He asks me if I was the one who recommended Demba for the position and I nod my head. He tells me that my family and I are under close watch and reminds me that treason is punishable by death. He waves me out of the room, but before I leave he tells me that his father will decide my fate.

Thunderstorms are a rarity, but the night after the execution of Demba, rain falls from the sky with no mercy. Sleep is hard to come by and I lay awake, Aminta resting her head on my chest. My mind is flooded with thoughts; what if Sulayman turns his wrath towards us? How would I protect us? There is nothing protecting us from the petty displeasure of Sulayman. My train of thought is broken as I hear horses splashing around in the mud and voices whispering outside. I peek my head out of the window and I feel the color, all of the blackness, leave my face. Ten soldiers are outside as one of them knocks on the door.

There is nothing I can do but open the door and accept whatever happens. When I open the door, I am instructed that Mansa Musa is back and wants to see Aminta and I. We are lead into one of the palace rooms, when we enter a string of doctors are huddled around Musa, who is mumbling words to them. Sagaman, Sulayman, Magha, and Fajr stand at a distance allowing the doctors to tend to Musa with complete concentration. Fajr and Aminta slowly gravitate to each other and exchange whispers among themselves. I am unsure if I have a friend in the room as I keep my distance, watching everyone in the room huddled and whispering.

"Prince Magha, a doctor should tend to your wounds," one of the doctors suggests.

"I'm fine, tend to father," Magha says. Fajr clicks her tongue and Magha comes to reason. "Fine, but make it quick," he submits, following the doctor into another room, guided by a slave holding a candle and two guards. In my lapse of focus, Sulayman has seemed to slip out of the room.

Sagaman slowly approaches me, "I do not, for one-second trust Sulayman," he confesses. "That is why I sent that message. I know for a fact you have your doubts as well," he whispers as the doctors continue doctoring.

"He had Demba put to death. No evidence and no trial," I say. Sagaman runs his hands over his face at the news and motions Fajr and Aminta to join us. As we all stand, exchanging information in the middle of the night, by candlelight, I wonder if this is what politics is truly about. Low whispers, candlelight, and strategy.

"He told me keeping me in my bed chambers was for my own protection," Fajr says. "I have not left the palace in weeks."

"Do we all truly think Sulayman and Al-Nasir worked together on this?" I ask. Everyone stays silent, slowly nodding in agreement.

"Mansa Musa, is asleep, we have applied ointment to his wounds and bandaged them. I think it would be best if we allowed him a good nights rest. Surely one of the first calm nights he has had in a few weeks," one of the doctors say. We exit the room and huddle outside in a hallway. When Aminta and I entered, the hall was not as heavily guarded as it is now.

Sagaman leans against the wall. There is a look in his face of deep thought and he commands the guards to the ends of the hall. "We shouldn't tell Musa any of this, at least, not so obviously. He will find out that Demba was executed and other events, but if we openly accuse Sulayman he will feel we are plotting," he says.

"Right, if we all attack Sulayman, his first instinct will be to protect his brother, we have to guide him to the right conclusion," Aminta adds. A strange feeling comes over me, a feeling like our lives just took a turn into a new direction, for the better or the worse, I am not yet sure.

"Aminta, Isa, please stay here the night, no need in traveling in the rain. You are more than welcome to stay in the palace tonight. You are welcome to stay," Fajr reaffirms our stay is welcome, but something in her voice says our stay is demanded. Sagaman snaps his finger and instructs guards to escort Aminta and I to our room. The sun will be up soon, and Aminta and I are wide awake.

"Isa," she says turning my head towards her and finding my eyes in the dark. "I never want to be afraid like that again in my life. I have spent the last few weeks wondering about our future. Do you have a plan?" I am speechless, never before as she been so blunt. I open my mouth to respond, but no sequence of words seems adequate. She kisses my chest, "I love you, and you know that, but your naivety can get us killed." She is right. Was this the shift I felt earlier? I turn to her and kiss her, savoring the taste of her lips, feeling the sweat on her upper lip caused by the humidity of the night.

"I promise, you will never be in the dark again," I kiss her lips again relishing in the feeling of her encompassing me. As we intertwine our bodies, enjoying the motions of each others hips, the sun leaks into the room, chasing the darkness away and spilling onto our black bodies.

It has been five years since Musa has taken the throne and two months since the attack on the army while on their way to Tagahza. Fajr has convinced Musa that I had been used by Demba in some grand scheme for a coup. There was no need to convince Musa otherwise, especially when everyone already believed it. Although, my soul is uneasy lying, whenever I was on the verge on telling the truth, I imagined the wrath of Musa if he thought I was lying. What if Sulayman was able to convince Musa I was lying? The image of Aminta having to watch me beheaded or even worse, having to watch her beheaded become a driving force behind my silence. I pray that there is some divine reward in telling a lie for the greater good. That maybe, for what I have done and for what I am going to do, divine justice will work through us and Allah's mercy will be gifted to us.

For now, Sagaman, Fajr, Aminta, and myself all agreed that it was Demba that planned the coup and Sulayman was the hero, not even Magha is in on our scheme. Magha, Musa, Sulayman, and the entire empire are mere specters, as I had been for years. We persuaded Musa to yield Tagahza to Al-Nasir, telling him to focus on the goldmines, and not one salt mine. But something happened after Musa completely recovered from his injuries, something we all saw coming, but for some reason too afraid to discuss. Musa became highly paranoid.

BOURÈ, MALI 1325

A paranoid ruler, with absolute power keeps everyone around him paranoid. Musa cheated death once and nothing could convince him that he was completely safe from the arrow or blade of an assassin. His paranoia became public policy as Musa now had an executioner on hand at all times. If he saw someone that looked guilty, a punishment could be handed down instantly. An arm, a hand, a finger, a head; whatever body part Musa felt was adequate was removed. What was more disheartening, for me at least, were the words of Demba. Demba told Musa that Bourè, was fine and well. Musa wanted to see his gold producing city run by slave labor for himself.

With only the power that he holds, Musa up and moved hundreds of people to Bourè, pitching tents, staying as close to the goldmines as possible. Once again, Musa appoints Sulayman as deputy, but this time I travel with Musa, Magha, and Segaman. Bourè, home of Musa's largest goldmines, is also home to a large kola nut market, not as lucrative as gold, but it is part of Musa's vast portfolio.

Segaman and Magha rode with the army securing trade routes around Bourè, looking for raiders, some of whom have come as far as North Africa. As they search and secure, Musa, in all his royal majesty and tapestry sits in a large white tent, surrounded by his loyal guards as slaves line up to present him with his own gold. He sits with his legs crossed, holds up each nugget, and inspects it for imperfections, which he has yet to find. While Musa inspects, I barter with merchants and slave traders for prices. People captured in the interior, were sent into slavery and the unlucky ones ended up here, working the goldmines.

"Mansa Musa would like to see you," a slave says peaking into my tent. I leave my maps and trade contracts, and follow the young slave into Musa's palace sized tent. Barrels of gold and other jewels are sprawled around the tent, Musa is sitting on the floor with an older woman in conversation. He introduces us, she is a dressmaker and he is sending her to Djenne and eventually to Timbuktu for business. She takes her leave and Musa hands me architect drawings.

"When we annex Timbuktu, this will be the school that Fajr and Aminta asked for, the school for girls, do you think they will like it?" I run my eyes over the massive plans, full with a courtyard, dining hall, and small market place for women merchants. "Everyday women merchants will set up their stands," Musa says standing over my shoulder and points to other points of interests. I want to ask why he has me dealing with trade contracts and not Sulayman, but I quickly remember my place.

"You have to take Timbuktu before any of this is possible," I say destroying Musa's moment of optimism.

"Yes, I know," he says while sighing, "I am making plans for a city that is not in my possession, but that will change. I want that city Isa. King Jarrah is hanging on to power by a thread. We need to focus on Timbuktu again." He takes the school plans from me and places them back on the table. "Everyone denies me Taghaza and I see everyone's argument, but I look weak. I gave up Tagahza, but I need a victory, I look like a failure." Musa in all is regality has a deep insecurity. I pass suggestions by him and he waves them off one by one.

"Father!" a voice shouts, which can only be one voice, Magha. He runs into the tent drenched in sweat. "We found a rebel group, thirty men, we have them a short ride from camp" he says.

"I told you!" Musa bellows, "I told you! Demba was not the only traitor, this runs deeper than him," he rants. Magha and Musa exit as I sit on the floor trying to collect myself for the pending drama. I can

57

hear Musa shouting orders from outside of the tent. "You, you, and all of you follow me. Take me to them!" I gather myself from the floor, find a horse, and follow the entourage. Magha was right, the ride was short, we arrive and thirty men are on their knees, hands behind their heads, in neat rows of five. Segaman greets us and tells us their findings. They found a group of men dressed in the same style as the attackers from the road to Tagahza. One of them confessed to being sent to kill Musa in exchange for his freedom. The rest of them kneel before Musa awaiting their fate.

Musa approaches the men and draws his sword. "Who sent you?" he says moving up and down the rows, dragging is sword behind him. He stops at one of them and places the sword against his throat. "Was it Al-Nasir? I bet it was Al-Nasir!" He moves to another one, "Jarrah, Jarrah sent you to kill me, didn't he! I tell you, I tell all of you, he knows I am coming for Timbuktu. This one here, kill him." Without question Musa's executioner drives his sword through the man's neck. "Umar, my brother in law, he killed his own brother and now he is coming for me, answer me!" The entire group continues to kneel in silence, ready to accept any fate that Musa is prepared to pass down.

As Musa moves from row to row, demanding answers, being met with silence he orders deaths, over and over again. I begin to wonder, what if Sulayman is innocent? Of course he is not completely innocent, but murdering his brother? Could Sulayman be so ambitious he would attempt to murder his brother twice?

"He is coming undone, look at him," Segaman whispers to me.

I nod in agreement. "You think he will kill all of them?"

"I have seen Musa order the death of an entire village. This is nothing to him," he says still whispering.

"An entire village?" I can feel my voice cracking trying to keep my whispers silent.

"They resisted paying tribute. Musa did not want to negotiate and was not feeling very merciful. He had all the men killed and sent the women and children into slavery," he says while Musa points to another assassin in the group to have a sword passed through his torso. Magha guides his horse towards Musa, whispers something in his ear and rides off.

"Send the rest to goldmines as slaves" Musa says coolly.

"Do you really still think Sulayman tried to kill Musa? Twice?" I ask.

"Even if he is innocent, can he be trusted?" Segaman asks before riding off to join Musa and Magha.

That night, images of children and women being sent to slavery and men killed, simply for resisting keeps me awake. I think back to seeing those people being carted into the city, along with gold and ivory, like they were mere things to be had and sold. The flap to my tent opens, and I can tell it is Musa from the figure in the candle light, he asks if I am awake in a loud whisper. I lift myself off the floor, but he tells me to keep comfortable as he moves a chair from the desk and places it by my mat. He tells me that he is unsure who can be trusted, but he is certain that Umar, King of Gao, his brother in law, tried to have him killed this time and the last time. He confesses that Demba might be innocent. Although, he did not order the death of Demba, he says it weighs heavy on his heart knowing an innocent man have been put to death. Musa cascades from Demba to the men he had killed and sent into slavery earlier today; saying how the situation demanded it.

"Am I becoming a tyrant?" he asks in a concerned voice. "The Qur'an warns against tyrants, you know. Pharaoh was a tyrant and Allah destroyed him." There is legitimate worry in Musa's voice.

"Pharaoh was not a Muslim nor did he heed the call to Allah."

"I wish being a Muslim absolved me of the sin of tyranny. The truth is, I want to rule Timbuktu, Gao, even Egypt, not because I feel I am a good ruler, because if I do not they will rule over me, over us," he says pointing to himself then to me. "I want the gold, the ivory, the salt, for no other reason than if it falls into the wrong hands, our lives could be over," he says. In this moment I realize Musa, just like the rest of us is fighting for survival.

"You do what you must, and in accordance to our religion" I respond.

Musa chuckles. "Religion," he says, "get some rest, we head home tomorrow. We also have to make plans for Ramadan. We will feed many people this year, not only at home but the entire kingdom will be provided suhoor and iftar," he says while leaving. The goal for the next few weeks is to make sure that Musa makes Magha deputy, not just for my sake, but for the sake of the empire.

As I climb onto my horse after a day of packing, readying for the return to Djenne, a cloud of dust approaches the camp site. Soldiers surrounded Musa and Magha as the rest of us are left to whatever pending danger approaches. Archers take aim at the cloud of dust, but as the cloud gets closer it is apparent it is a messenger with urgent news. Musa instructs a group of soldiers to meet the messenger and inquire about his purpose. Their voices are out of range for any of us to hear, but a solider points to me and the messenger gallops over to me and hands me a folded piece of paper. Musa walks over to me as I am sure he saw the color from my face drain.

"What is it? Bring water! And a chair!" he commands. I feel my knees become heavy and weak at the same time. I hand the paper to Musa as he looks it over. Aminta was carrying a child, but heavy bleeding terminated the pregnancy. My father in law, Dawud died from the sleeping sickness. I stand up from the chair and tell Musa we should start heading back while we have sunlight.

DJENNE, MALI 1325

"Ramadan starts tomorrow!" little voices yell, shouting over the high walls of each house, grabbing the attention of anyone who will listen. I have been in correspondence with Ambassador Ebrima while he has also been in correspondence with Musa. Embrima has persuaded Musa to visit Cairo on the way to Mecca this year. Musa has told us that the trip is simply religious, as he wants to meet the famed scholars of Al-Azhar and local clerics. He has no desire to meet with, "That greedy Sultan" as he calls Al-Nasir. Al-Nasir, extended an official invitation to visit his palace, but Musa refuses time and time again.

Since the failed assassination attempt at Bourè, Musa has quietly been plotting to annex Timbuktu, it seems he is simply waiting for a reason to attack King Jarrah. Umar has denied in writing to Fajr that he had any parts of either attempts on Musa's life. The love Fajr bares for her brother is great as she swears by Allah that she believes he is telling the truth. There is still the problem of Sulayman, who has been very quite as of late. No complaining, no tantrums, no hands around my neck. His son, Qasa has become head of the treasury, occupying the role of Demba. I'm unsure if the choice was Musa's or Sulayman's.

That may change soon, Fajr has been working in private trying to persuade Musa to name Magha deputy when we go on Hajj. I have watched Musa ignore Fajr's advice on many occasions. The only fact that calms my nerves is that she was able to convince Musa on building the girl's school in Timbuktu. Although construction has not started and Musa has no authority in Timbuktu, he is simply waiting like a snake stalking its prey.

Before the start of Ramadan, Musa had enough gold sent to the various provinces in the empire to provide food for the month of

Ramadan. Now that that Ramadan is upon us, I hope to leave the politics behind me, if only for a month. A knock at my office door interrupts my daydreaming as Aminta moves some papers from my desk and places a cup of tea on my desk.

"Where are the boys?" I ask her.

"At the library with Ahmed Baba, they are studying Al-Ghazali this week," she says. "They're almost men now," her voice breaks and she places her hands over her eyes, trying her best to stop the tears from flooding down her face.

"I know you miss him. I cannot find the words to express how sorry I am for missing the janaza." Aminta wipes the few droplets from her eyes that managed to escape and gives me a smile.

"I know, Isa, I know. Father lived a long and fulfilling life. We must make sure the boys stay on course," she says. "Are we going on hajj this year? I have heard rumors that Musa wants to make a stop in Cairo before Mecca?"

I pull out letters from Embrima and hand them to her. "Musa has been sending funds to Cairo to construct housing and food kitchens for pilgrims coming from Mali in Cairo," I say proudly. She hands me the letters and takes a seat on my lap.

"Does it bother you I could never give you children?" Her question catches me off guard. I want to tell her the truth, but the truth would not be helpful to anyone right now. I wrap my arms around her and kiss her forehead.

"It was the will of Allah. Look at the life we have built for ourselves. I'd rather be right here with you just as you are, I love you." Since the night Musa returned from Tagahza, I have found lying to be a lot easier than before. The Prophet said that truthfulness leads to righteousness and righteousness leads to paradise. I hope Allah can forgive me for the endless lies that I have told. That we all have told these last few years. In the life that I have been placed into, I have learned that deception is part of survival.

After duhr I walk to the palace for the last council meeting before Ramadan. As I am walking through the market, Yusuf ibn Said waves me down, from the bookseller's stand.

"As-salaam-laykum, Isa, you headed to the council meeting too?"

"Wa-laykum-salaam," I respond giving him a friendly hug, although, after all these years I can't say we are friends. "I am. I see you picked up yet another book."

"Yes, we must seek knowledge, it is a command from Allah Himself," he says loud enough for the entire market to hear. A gentle reminder to the good people of Djenne. "Have you noticed something, off, about Mansa Musa?" he asks. I stop.

"Off? How do you mean?"

"Yesterday night, he came to my room. He asked me, what does it mean to govern Islamcially. I was unsure if he wanted to talk about the entire concept of sharia while sitting on the foot of my bed or if he wanted a quick answer" he says.

"Yusuf," I look him in the eye and I can feel my heart begin to race, "what did you tell him?" I say clinching my teeth. A grimace passes his face as he pulls away from my grip, a grip that I hadn't noticed I applied.

"All I did was give him a book," he says while trying to figure out where my aggression came from. I apologize and attribute my behavior to a lack of sleep and stress, the pressures of governing

64

have been getting to me I tell him. He accepts my apology and we walk to the palace, exchanging small talk about our families and recent books we have read.

"We are going to need more gold than that," Musa tells Qasa, pacing the room, while the rest of the council members listen to the plans for the journey to Cairo. "We are going to show the world the power of this empire by giving away the very thing that makes us powerful, gold." Musa says, pacing around the table. "I want people to admire the wealth we have here, to attract merchants far and wide. I want to bring scholars to this empire from all the lands in which the Qur'an is recited and held dear." Musa adjusts one of the rings on his finger. "Everyone here has a job to do in order to make this a success, truly a joint effort," he says.

Musa takes his seat at the head of the council table and lets out a deep sigh. "I have heard all of your news and you have heard mine. There is the matter of deputy. Sulayman, make no mistake you are still heir to the throne, but you will be needed in Cairo more than Djenne. Magha will act as deputy in my place."

Sulayman looks indifferent to the news as if he and Musa already had this very discussion. Musa stands up as we all stand and bow. "Ramadan Mubarak," he says and takes his leave. In all honesty I was expecting a more dramatic scene from Musa and Sulayman both, but the problem remains, Sulayman is next in line to the throne.

During Ramadan the courtyard of the palace was used to feed the hungry diplomats, courtiers, council members, and the royal family. After isha and with the moon in full view, the mosque fills with people praying taraweh. Some have spent the night in the mosque especially during these last few nights of Ramadan. Sometimes entire families would spend the night in the masjid for the chance to dedicate more time to prayer and reflection.

I take a few kola nuts from the table outside of the entrance hall of the palace mosque. These long days would not be possible without the help of these nuts. I hear footsteps marching in rhythm which can only mean Musa is close by with his guards. Musa turns the corner into the courtyard and spots me. "Take as many as you need," he says popping a few kola nuts into his mouth. "You know, I have been reading this book ibn Said gave me, 'Islamic Laws for Governance and Ethics.'" I raise my eyebrows to show my interest and he motions me to sit on the bench. From the bench the call for the start of taraweh starts. Musa ignores it and keeps talking about the book he is reading.

"Jarrah had a masjid in Timbuktu destroyed," he says calmly. "During Ramadan, can you believe it?" Musa gazes up at the stars as if he is looking for an answer to shoot across the night sky. Musa has been stalking Timbuktu for years and now he has the exact reason to coil his grip around the city.

"This is what you wanted. A reason to take Timbuktu?" I say in a moment of misguided honesty.

"You think I wanted a masjid to be torn to the ground? Muslims unable to pray during Ramadan? I am many things Isa, but heartless is not one of them." Musa stands up and takes a few steps forward, gazes at the stars again, then sits back down. "Politically, yes it does work in my favor, but that is the very thing I am struggling with. What I have to do politically as a leader most times conflicts with what I am supposed to do as a Muslim. I have to make decisions, daily, that do not have simple answers." Musa runs four fingers through his beard and looks at me. "The older I get the more I think about how I will be held accountable for everything I do by Allah."

66

"So, does this mean you won't annex Timbuktu?" I ask. Musa looks at me and laughs so hard I can see his back teeth as he tilts his head back.

"No, no, no, Timbuktu will be part of my empire. If I do not, then someone else will snatch it. The approach I have in mind will be more diplomatic. We can achieve our goals without force, inshaAllah," he says patting my knee. "We will give out food and gold to the people, Muslim and non Muslim alike," Musa says.

"Let us head inside. Keeping Allah waiting seems haram," he says comically. As the imam is reciting the Qur'an, I find it hard to focus on the words being recited. All the people that I have been watching these past few years are once again in the same room. It is only during salaah that we are all in the same room while being quite. This is not the first time Ramadan or taraweeh, but something feels different. There is a tension in the air, as if everyone is suspicious of everyone. Nobody in this room can be trusted, yet we all share such a sacred space.

I am shoulder to shoulder with Musa and in all my years I have never seen him cry during prayer. He is not sobbing uncontrollably, but his cry is that of someone who has a heavy heart. Who has been walking around in this life with deeds that the angels have written on his record that cannot be expunged. There has never been a time that I have thought to pray for Musa's soul. The idea of needing to make dua for him seems foreign. What he said earlier tonight, about having to make decisions that have no simple answers. Killing and enslaving an entire village, as Musa has done, maybe he should be crying uncontrollably.

Chests of silk, gold walking sticks, and other luxury goods flood into the city and are placed into the courtyard of the palace.

As the days of Eid passed, I and many others finalized plans for the journey which Musa said may take up to two years. Ambassador Embrima wrote to me telling me that the housing in Cairo was complete and that there is much talk in the court of Al-Nasir about Musa's visit. The road from Djenne to Cairo and many surrounding roads are occupied by the military. The route from Cairo to Mecca has been "left to the will of Allah," in Musa's own words. The only people staying in Djenne, were Magha and Ahmed Baba, one being too old to leave, the other too important to leave.

As the caravan is forming to leave Djenne, people stand to witness eighty camels carrying three hundred pounds of gold each form a straight line. Slaves adorned in silk and their gold walking sticks lined up chatting in excitement. Segaman reviews his troops who will escort the caravan until we reach Cairo. Al-Nasir was very clear he would not allow any armed men in Cairo. Only a few trained soldiers will be with us in Cairo, but Al-Nasir promised us the best of protection.

Magha exchanges hugs and kisses with Fajr and Musa as the caravan slowly moves forwards to leave the city. I can hear Musa tell Magha that the matter of his marriage will be settled, as he and Fajr will look to forge a relationship with royalty outside of the empire. Possibly a governor of Al-Nasir will be interested in marrying his daughter to a prince of the Mali Empire. As the sun shines down on us I look over at Aminta and kiss her forehead. A slave offers us water and I decline and suggest he drink it. Musa and Fajr's carriage is directly in front of us. As we start to pick up speed, Musa turns to me and asks if I had messengers placed along the roads of our journey. I nod my head and tell him communication between, Djenne and Cairo was settled, but there was lack of communication between Mecca and Djenne. He laughs and says maybe, it will be good to loose communication for a while. Any issues that arise Magha can handle it. He has full Mansa authority. As the caravan approached Cairo, we exchange the mud brick structures of Djenne for the stone buildings of Cairo.

We entered the city in the dead of night, but Ambassador Embrima was well prepared for us. Musa, tired from the journey, suggested we all head to the housing complex he had built, which included stables and various courtyard, all the luxuries of home. As thousands of slaves found their rooms. Embrima notified Musa that their may not be enough room for seven thousand slaves, and he suggested some camp outside of city gates. As I close the door to our room, Embrima whispers my name in the dark hallway. I look over my shoulder and Aminta is already sound asleep in bed.

I close the door behind me and he motions me closer. His mouth is so close to my ear I can feel the stubble of his beard on my face even though we are not touching. He tells me some information is too sensitive to be written down and that the crown prince of Egypt, Al-Jashnakir wants to meet with me. As he pulls his face away from my ear he says in a low voice that it is imperative that Musa and Al-Nasir meet face to face. Even more unsettling, Musa is going to have to kiss his feet in front of the entire Egyptian court. I have no choice but to laugh at such an outrages request, but Ebrima's face is unmoved. He is serious.

CAIRO, EGYPT 1325

"Where is Musa?" I ask one of the passing slaves as I stick my head out of my door, peeking into the hallway.

"Mansa Musa has left for the day to attend lectures at Al-Azhar." I nod as if I had simply forgotten that vital piece of information, but in reality I had no idea where Musa was. I head outside of the housing complex and the busy streets of Cairo greet me with passing merchants, not so different from Djenne, except less black people.

"Isa!" Embrima waves as he hands me a horse and tells me to follow him. We make our way down the various paved roads until we reach a house on a not so busy street. Embrima sees my hesitation, and gives me a friendly push into the doorway.

A man in a long purple robe is sitting at a table with a sword laying on the table. His hair is black with streaks of gray. "As salaam-al-laykum," he says, "I'm Al-Jashnakir," he says while extending his hand. I take his hand and return his salaam, I begin to introduce myself, but he stops me. "I know who you are, Isa, the Chief of Mansa Musa's council." I smile nervously at the idea of being known outside of Mali. He invites us to sit and asks about the journey from Djenne.

After courteous small talk, I grow impatient. "So, why am I here?"

Al-Jashnakir nods as if he is impressed with my forwardness. "Isa, we have a mutual problem." I raise my eyebrows and look over at Embrima who avoids my gaze. "A certain merchant from Venice. Mr. Girando de Parma."

"The paper merchant? What about him?"

"Well, he is not just a paper merchant. He is here in Cairo and has been since he left Djenne," Embrima says. "Who introduced Girando do Musa?" he asks.

"Sulayman," I say trying to follow the up coming connection he was about to make.

"And who was left out of the deal that Girando offered?" Al-Jashnakir asks.

"…Sulayman," I reply.

Al-Jashnakir pushes away from the table and stands up. "Girando, has been advising Al-Nasir on economic policy for a while now. A policy that is very, pro European. And I need him gone and so do you."

"Does Girando know that we are here?" I ask.

"Yes, and he is expecting a gift from Musa in the form of gold for being such a good business partner," Ebrima says.

"This is where it gets a little haram," Al Jashnakir says. "I need you, well not you personally, but I need him eliminated," he says while running his hand over his neck. "You will take him a wagon of gold, a wagon that will also hide your unarmed soldiers, who will be given arms." Al-Jashnakir unsheathes a sword hidden behind his back and plays with it as the sunlight bounces off of the blade, sending the reflection to different corners of the room.

"Why would I do this? This seems like I am doing you a favor and getting nothing in return," I reply bluntly.

"In his home you will find exactly what you need to fix the little problem you have with Sulayman. You want him out of the succession? No?" he asks as if he already knows my answer.

71

"You have my attention," I say.

"All that you need will be in his office. We both want and need him dead, but this cannot be connected to me," Al-Jashnikr says.

"Do not worry, I will take care of that. But, why does Musa have to bow to Al-Nasir?" I ask.

"That is for me. Call it a political victory," he says.

"You want Mansa Musa, who walked into this city with more gold than is in the ground of all of North Africa to bow to a ruler who lost power, twice? He would never," I say waving my hand in the air dismissing his nonsense. "You're asking me to basically persuade Musa to embarrass himself in from of the Malian and Egyptian court. Killing Girando is easy, Musa will never kiss the feet of Al-Nasir."

"Either Musa kisses the feet of Al-Nasir or Girando's influence grows here in Cairo and I will not have that!" Al-Jashnakir gathers himself after temporarily losing his temper. "Sulayman will be next to the throne and you will not survive that. Who knows when these assassins will actually hit Musa win an arrow or blade? Make it happen Isa." I nod in agreement, thinking of how terrified I was when Sulayman had a brief moment of power. "Good, I have a few meetings to attend, one of which happens to be with Sulayman," Al-Jashnakir says while standing up to leave.

"Wait," I say in a voice that sounded more demanding that suggestive. Embrima shoots me a look of concern as I am about to veer off script. Al-Jashnakir turns around and opens his arms. "I want Taghaza back in Malian control."

"Isa..." Embrima says, but I hold my hand out to silence him. "Make my job a little easier in convincing Musa. Give us something more in return other than the death of a mutual enemy."

Al-Jashnakir chuckles and points to me. "I thought you were a political novice, but here you are putting me in a very tough position," he says while sitting back down at the table. "I can promise you a conversation with Al-Nasir about Tagahza, if Musa meets with him."

"Do not forget that Tagahza is rightfully property of Mansa Musa," I say as Al-Jashnakir leaves.

"It belongs to whoever collects taxes there, which is Al-Nasir," he says without turning around, leaving Embrima and I alone.

Embrima and I sit in the empty house for a few moments in silence when I turn to him and ask if Sulayman knows Girando has been in Cairo this entire time. Embrima raises his eyebrows, silently confirming what was always known, Sulayman is not as innocent as he portrays and the proof is in Cairo. "We are only here for two more days, confirm the plan with Al-Jashnakir and have a letter sent to Girando that you and I are delivering a gift to him. On our last day in Cairo, I'll persuade Musa to meet with Al-Nasir. By the time Girando is found we will be in Mecca."

As I approach the housing complex, Musa is dressed in all white, talking to a North African man also dressed in all white. "Where have you been?" Musa asks while embracing me. I lie and say the markets. "I just heard the most amazing lecture on the importance of sadaqah. For so long I have sent others to distribute charity for me, missing out on the blessing of giving to the needy with my own hands." Musa looks down at his hands, takes a ring from his finger and gives it to the next person that passes by. "There is a white thobe in your room, we are going to give out sadaqah in the streets today, just us," he says. Without protest I go to my room and change. When

I return, Musa has two bags of gold, he hands me one and we make our way into the busy and narrow streets of Cairo.

After ten minutes of handing out gold nuggets and saying bismillah each time, I realize this is the first time I have seen Musa without any guards surrounding him. We hand gold to women, children, men, Christians, Muslims, and Jews. Moving from street to street, trying to find those who may seem less fortunate, but who isn't less fortunate than Mansa Musa?

"You there!" a voice from behind shouts, I turn around to see two Egyptian guards with their hands gripping the handle of their swords. I tap Musa, but he is immersed in conversation with a man on the street. The two guards walk towards us. "You two, black men, what is in those bags!"

Musa ends his conversation and turns to the guards and tells them the bags are filled with gold. He opens the bag and shows it to them.

"And where did you get this gold?" asks the guard who has a birthmark that runs from the bottom of his nose to the bottom of his chin. I wonder if Musa is going to say he is the ruler of the Mali Empire or if he Is going to lie. Musa and I stand in silence. "So you stole it?" the guard without the birthmark suggests. Musa and I deny his claim, stumbling and stuttering over our words.

"There has been many assaults and robberies in the area. You two are just walking the streets of Cairo with bags of gold?" The guard with the birthmark reveals his sword and motions for Musa to place the strap of the bag on the blade. I do the same.

The guard without the birthmark demands that we never show our face in Cairo again, in fact he suggests that we leave Cairo as soon as we can. Musa and I walk back in silence. Musa, his entire life, has never had anything taken from him, he has always been the taker. These two guards pulled their swords and left Musa speechless, possibly afraid. After this, asking him to kiss the feet of Al-Nasir will be twice as hard.

"How was your day?" I ask Aminta as she climbs into bed snuggling next to me.

"A lot of walking, Fajr and I went to different soup kitchens, many needed repairs so we gave them funds to fix them. I have a feeling people here have never seen a black person with such wealth." I motion for her to put her feet up. "Wait! I purchased this cream in the market today, it is supposed to make the skin softer. The lady said Cleopatra herself used this same cream."

I take the cream and rub it on her foot, massaging it into her skin. "Musa and I were robbed today by Egyptian guards."

"Did they hurt you?" she asks.

"Not at all, they just wanted our gold. I guess Al-Nasir underpays his soldiers." After a few moments of silence, I clear my throat. "Musa has to meet with Al-Nasir," I say while taking her other foot in my hand and applying the cream.

"Musa has made it very clear that this journey is not political, simply religious," Aminta replies.

"For Musa, the religious and the political are one and the same. Not only does he has to meet him, but bow to him and kiss his feet."

While laughing at the possible sight of Musa bowing to another human she asks why. I explain the meeting with Al-Jashnakir, Girando being in Cairo, having to kill him, and possible evidence against Sulayman. Aminta reminds me that we are only in Cairo for a few days, therefore anything that must be done, must be done quickly.

"Are we going to Timbuktu after we leave Mecca?" she asks.

"It seems that way. Musa will not be denied any longer," I say kissing her forehead.

"And we will have our girls school?"

"You won't be denied either," I say tapping her foot signaling the end of her massage.

"Do you think Musa will agree to meet him if it means he could get back Taghaza?" I ask.

"Meet him? Yes, Kiss his feet? In front of his wife, his brother, the entire Egyptian court? You have a giant task ahead of you," she replies.

Day 2

After Asr, Musa and I find ourselves roaming the streets, this time with unarmed soldiers with us. I confess to Musa, Aminta's inability to have children. He asks if we have seen a doctor. I reveal we have seen many doctors, but none have been able to help us. Musa suggests adoption and I tell him it is a thought that has passed in our minds before. Musa stops in the middle of the street and points to a church.

"I have read a few books on Christianity, but never have I seen a church," Musa says while approaching the door. I follow him and out of respect or maybe ignorance we remove our shoes at the door. An old man with light skin and a heavy cross dangling from his neck greets us with salaam, and invites us to sit. Musa asks the man if he is a priest and the man nods his head yes.

"Tell me of your religion," Musa asks.

"What do you want to know?" the old man replies.

"Jesus, I have tried, I really have, to understand Jesus in your religion, but I fall short every time," Musa explains.

"God became man so man can become God," the priest says pointing a golden statue of a man hanging from a cross. "In fact it was in Egypt where Bishop Clement said those famous words."

The last thing one should tell a ruler with the power of Musa that he could become God. Musa grins at the priest. "That sounds absolutely ridiculous," Musa says exposing all of his teeth while laughing. We all share a laugh, but the priest's smile disappears first.

"Religion is supposed to be a bit ridiculous, right?" says the priest.

"What do you mean?" I ask.

"We both believe in the Virgin Birth, do we not?" Musa and I nod our heads in unison. "Does the story of Jesus, which we both share certain aspects of, sound a bit ridiculous? In your book, he speaks from the cradle!" The priest lets out a loud laugh. "Yet, you both believe in Islam as much as I believe in Christianity."

"So which one is right?" I ask.

The priest frantically shakes his head. "See this is the problem with your generation, you want to be right about everything. Religion is not about being right. It is about being better, as a person," he says while pointing to Musa and I. "How can we be right when by our very human nature, we are flawed? That is the question you need to you ask yourself."

Musa looks at me and then the priest. "This is what I needed to hear," Musa says while sarcastically laughing pointing at the priest in jest.

"Where are you two from?" the priest asks.

"Mali," I reply. The priest holds out his arms to signal the size of the Mali Empire and to be more specific.

"Djenne," Musa says.

"I have heard great things about the leader of Mali. I think he is roaming Cairo as we speak. I hear he is supposed to meet with Al-Nasir. What a political spectacle that would be!" Musa slowly turns his head to me as the priest, with all his might, stands up. "You two stay as long as you wish," the priests pats us on our heads and slowly walks out of the church.

"Is there something you wish to tell me, Isa," Musa says through his teeth in the form of a statement and not a question.

"Al-Nasir sent the crown prince, Al-Jashnakir to talk to me about you meeting him." Musa remains silent so I continue. "He wants you to submit yourself before him, bow, and kiss his feet."

The chair that Musa was sitting in suddenly soars across the room and breaks against the church wall. "I did not travel through the desert to kiss the feet of anyone! All I asked of you was to keep politics away from me for a month! A month!" he shouts. "And now, you are asking me to kiss the feet of Al-Nasir? In front of my wife? My brother? The entire damn Egyptian court!" Musa lifts up another chair and sends it across the room. The chair shatters against the golden statue of Jesus. The statue, teeters back and forth and eventually falls to the floor, sending Jesus' head rolling across the floor.

The last time I saw Musa this angry, he slapped me and banished me from court. I need a flood of honesty to calm his temper. "I told Al-Jashnakir I would talk to you, only if he would agree to give us

Taghaza back. I know the insult is great, but Musa, the benefit is even greater!"

Musa grabs me by the front of my thobe and his eyes grow wide. "You wish to put a price on my dignity? In a country we were robbed in!" I break away from his grip and shove him. Musa stumbles, but catches his balance.

"If you want to let your pride get in the way, fine! I have done nothing, nothing but try to help you, from day one! You want slaves and I get you slaves. You want a village and I get you a village. You want a new palace and I get you a new palace. I literally live for you Musa! The entire empire lives to serve you!"

"Please, Isa, spare me the tears. If it was up to you, you would still be living as a single man in a hut. I practically had to hold you hostage to get you out of that miserable life." We both stand in silence digesting each others bitter truth. Musa lowers his head. "So, what is in it for you?"

My first reaction is to deny being selfish, but lying seems more fitting. I know I can keep whatever information about Sulayman a secret for now, but Tagahza has already been revealed. "I wanted it to seem like I was responsible for a political victory in Tagahza," I say in false shame.

Musa paces the aisles of the church. A few worshippers enter the doorway while Musa's back is turned and I motion for them to leave. Whatever prayer they were about to say is not more important than the words about to come out of Musa's mouth. The future of empires depended on Musa's thoughts, they can pray to Jesus somewhere else.

"I will do it, but I want a meeting with him afterwards. Me, you, Al-Nasir, and Jashnakir." I hide my smile by simply nodding and turning to leave the church. The fact that Musa did not name

Sulayman brings me a sliver of joy. "You are the first person to ever put their hands on me in that way since I was crowned." I turn to face him. "You do it again and I cannot promise I will be so calm." Musa looks down at the head of Jesus which is at his feet and kicks it.

Day 3

Before sunrise, Embrima and I load a wagon with gold. We recruit six soldiers and demand their secrecy. I tell them, sometimes Mansa Musa needs to be in the dark on issues for the empire to run smoothly. After Dhur we take the wagon to the same empty house we met Al-Jashnakir in to pick up the swords, bows, and arrows that we requested. Girandino hires former Egyptian soldiers as his personal guards. They will check the wagon, but not thoroughly, not with this much gold coming through. Our soldiers hide in the trap compartment of the wagon, and just like we thought, the guards let us through without question.

Girando's house, a stone fortress on the Nile, is away from any sort of civilization and a long ride away from the commotion of the city. Girando looks down on us from his balcony and tells us the door will be open in a moment. Girando motions for us to come in as two black slaves usher us inside. When we enter, I am taken aback at the scenery, the sun shining above the Nile. The white curtains dance in the breeze. A black slave offers us a drink, Embrima puts the cup to his lip but, he puts the cup back on the tray. "Its wine," he says while a look of disgust passes through his face.

When Girando looks at me and points to the slave who offered me a drink. "You know each other?" Girando asks while taking the cup I declined and gulping it down. I shake my head no, but the young man does look a bit familiar. "I have not seen you in ages," Girando says while reclining on one of the large pillows on the floor. A black slave comes by and offers us figs which we gladly take. "Embrima and I have become somewhat of good friends, isn't that right?" Embrima responds with a nod as he fills his mouth with a fig.

"Why have you not returned to Venice?" I ask.

"Return to Venice? What is there to return to? War and famine is all I have known in Venice. I came to Cairo after I left Djenne and I simply fell in love!"

Girando regales us with stories about his travels through Libya and Morocco. He tells us how great the food is, but the women are even better. He loved the women there so much that he purchased a few at a slave auction. While he is talking he is enjoying cup after cup of wine. After two hours of entertaining Girando's stories, four black figures emerge from around the corner of the sitting room. They creep towards Girando as his back is turned to them. Embrima and I sit still as the four soldiers communicate in silence. They inching towards Girando, deciding which one of them will do the deed. The slaves stand in silence, I can only imagine their cynical gratification. As Girando calls for more wine, in his slurred speech, one solider covers Girando's mouth and the other strangles him. His face turns red as we all watch the life literally leave his body.

"Are the guards dead?" Embrima asks.

"Yes, sir," one of the soldiers says. One of the soldiers who is armed with a bow and arrow, quickly knots his bow and takes aim.

"Wait!" I yell lowering his bow with my hand. "How much have you seen?" I ask the stranger. A young woman with dark brown skin and a curly. She has a black robe wrapped around her.

"What will happen to me now that he is dead? I presume that he is, dead," she says peaking at Girando's body. "There is no way I can go to another slave auction! I will do anything!" The young woman starts to disrobe when Embrima stops her.

"That, will not be necessary," he says, motioning her to put her robe back on.

"What is your name," I ask

"Samira," she says.

"Where are you from Samira?"

"My father is from Morocco and my mother was a black slave from Mali," she says. "But I grew up in Morocco." I nod, and thank her for sharing her story.

"Samira, show me Girando's office," I demand. She takes me down the hall and up a flight of stairs where papers are stacked on his desk. As I start rummaging through the papers I realize that I have no idea what I am looking for. Embrima enters the office and aimlessly starts tossing around papers. After almost an hour of searching I stumble across a letter from Sulayman to Girando. The letter details Musa's plan to march to Tagahza. There is another letter from Sulayman detailing Musa's plan to visit Bouré. As I shuffle through the pile of letters, I find a letter from Umar to Girando, thanking him for the information on Musa's march to Tagahza. Another letter apologizes for the failed attempt on Musa's life, but he is sure that many chances will be had. Umar tells Girando. In another letter Umar says that if Fajr discovers his plan she would be crushed, but would forgive him.

I hand the letters to Embrima as he looks over them and hands them back to me. The soldiers have gathered all the slaves in the house, including Samira. The looks on their face ranged from, "Kill me now" to "you're going to have to kill me now."

"What do we do with them?" Embrima asks.

I go over all the possibilities of having six people who witnessed what happened living in Egypt. "Leave the bodies of the guards, it makes it look like a robbery. Escort the slaves, back to Djenne, put them under the care of Prince Magha. Take the gold back to Djenne as well, when we get back all of you will have freedom and gold, in exchange for your silence," I say.

They gather themselves off of the floor and shuffled out of the door. I turn to Embrima, "We have to tell Segaman."

"Who is going to tell Musa?" Embrima asks. I sigh at the fact of having to deliver news that his brother and brother-in-law have tried to kill him. Not only that, we have to make it to Mecca and back, and who knows what information Sulayman has sent out into the world and to who.

As the moon comes into view, Segaman, Embrima, and I sit in a newly renovated bathhouse. The building is guarded by Egyptian guards, granted to us by Al-Jashnakir. "Do you know what Sulayman and Qasa have been involved in while we have been here?" I ask Segaman.

"Trade deals mostly. He has been looking for a new partner to bring to Musa for a deal on cotton and other linen," Segaman says while splashing his feet in the water.

"What do you think Musa will do?" Embrima asks.

"Most likely, he would want to move troops to Gao, but that would be hard to do with Musa here," Segaman says.

"He is going to write to Magha and have him move troops for him," I respond.

"And Sulayman?" I ask. Embrima and Segaman fall silent, both looking at their reflection in the water. "We basically have two rival

83

successions, as of now, Sulayman and Qasa are all in line. These letters could change all of that," I say.

"I would not mind if Musa decided to execute Sulayman. That is the punishment for treason, is it not? The same punishment that Demba received?" Segaman says.

I tilt my head back and inhale deeply. "So much depends on tomorrow, I just have to find the right time to tell him."

Musa wanted Timbuktu and Gao, with these letters and the destruction of the masjid in Timbuktu, he can have both. Sulayman could also be removed if everything comes together perfectly.

Day 4

Musa steps outside in an all white throbe, which has been his uniform during the entire trip, a show of modesty no doubt. I have not seen Yusuf ibn Said since we arrived, but he shuffles his feet and joins us. When we arrive to the Amir Alin Aq Palace, the high stone walls and reflective marble floors welcome us. The long entrance hall is occupied with rows of soldiers standing as still as statues. Al-Jashnakir greets us, as he shakes hands with each of us one by one. Aminta and I enter the palace hand in hand admiring the newly built palace. Musa's slow and rhythmic pace slows us all down as he takes his time walking the grand hallway.

All of a sudden Musa stops and turns to one of the statue like soldiers. Musa steps to the man, steps closer, then takes the man's face. Musa scans the man's face.

"You stole from me," Musa says. He waves me over, "This is the man, no?" I nod in agreement gazing upon his birthmark. Al-Jashnakir looks on curiously as Musa unsheathes the man's sword. "Yusuf, what is the punishment for theft in Mali?" Musa asks sarcastically.

84

"Repayment of the goods that were stolen," Yusuf says.

Musa balances the tip of the blade on his finger, "And the punishment for theft from the Mansa?"

"Death," Yusuf says. The man breaks his statue like trance to plead for his life but to no avail. With one stroke Musa cuts open the man's throat. As the man falls to his knees holding his neck, Musa backs away to ensure no blood is spilled on his white thobe.

"Someone clean this up. We have to hurry Mansa Musa does not have all day," Al-Jashnakir says pointing to people to remove the body. We enter the throne room, and Al-Nasir is sitting on his throne. Diplomats, intellectuals, courtiers, and, merchants of the empire watch as we enter. We all bow to Al-Nasir as custom and Musa approaches the throne. Musa places one foot in front of the other and climbs the few steps to Al-Nasir. A pillow is placed before Musa as he kneels on the pillow. Al-Nasir removes his silk slippers and exposes his aged feet.

Musa pauses, takes a foot in each hand, and kisses each foot. Al-Nasir cannot contain his grin as he lifts his frail body from his throne. A servant rushes over and hands him a gold walking stick. "The Great Mansa Musa of Mali!" Al-Nasir says sarcastically as the room erupts. Applause, laughter, cheers, and gasps can all be heard. Musa stands and looks at us, the only black faces in the room besides the slaves. In this moment I realized this was not just about Mali, but the color of our skin. Al-Nasir motions for Musa to follow him as Al-Jashnakir motions me to follow. We are lead into a room with a table filled with fruit, bread, and pitchers of water.

Al-Nasir struggles to sit as he places walking stick on the table. "Do you think your brother tried to kill you?" Al-Nasir asks Musa brashly. "Why else would you have him here unless you wanted to keep an eye on him."

I shift in my chair nervously, curious as to how much Al-Nasir knows or if he is making a political observation that I missed. Musa smirks, as he takes a pitcher of water and washes his mouth out. Musa spits the water on the floor then grabs a piece of bread. "He is more useful here with me than in Djenne," Musa says coolly.

"Right, so now that you have submitted yourself before me, what is there to talk about? Oh right, Tagahza, you want your salt mine back," Al-Nasir says while making himself comfortable in his large wooden chair. Musa tosses the bread on the floor.

Al-Jashnakir chimes in, "I am sure we can come to a suitable agreement for both of our empires."

"You can keep Tagahza, it means very little to me. The price is a marriage between one your daughters to my son, Prince Magha."

Al-Nasir nudges Al-Jashnakir playfully. He laughs so hard he begins to cough. His old lungs cannot handle the work of comedy it seems. I wish Musa would have told me of his plan earlier, so we could look united, but how can I fault him for being dishonest? The very reason we are sitting in a room with Al-Nasir is because of my dishonesty, which to me is simply good politics.

"I must be honest with you, Musa. Egypt, looks to the south of our border for slaves. Not spouses," Al-Nasir says.

"Salt and gold too, your majesty," I cut in as Al-Jashnakir nods in agreement with my statement.

"If I marry one of my daughters to you, my people will not understand. An Egyptian marrying a Malian? Unheard of," Al-Nasir says.

"Listen, this is not personal," Al-Jashnakir pleads. "Egyptians here at court are very conservative with these types of matters. They would see such as union a form of weakness."

Al-Nasir looks between Musa and I. "In one year's time my tax collectors and military will leave Tagahza and it is all yours." Al-Jashnakir looks as if he wants to comment, but he comes to his senses and stays silent, careful not to disagree with his sultan in public. I was hoping for some good news to dampen the inevitable bad news I have yet to deliver to Musa.

Musa stands and I stand too. He walks towards the door and I follow. He turns around and looks at Al-Nasir and Al-Jashnakir. "As the Qur'an says, 'be not like those who abused Musa.' You keep Tagahza."

I try to keep up with Musa who is walking at a fast pace down the empty hall of the palace. When I catch up to him, I grab him by the shoulder. He turns to me with tears in his eyes. "Four days we have been here and four days I have been shown nothing but disrespect," he says in a whisper, careful of his surroundings. Even empty halls have ears.

"I know, I have tried everything in my power to shield you from all of this," I say as Musa wipes tears from his face. I take the letters from Girandino's office out of my pocket and hand it to him. Musa goes over each one, folds the letters, and places them in his pocket.

"I will not ask how you got these," Musa says while continuing to walk out the palace. When we arrive back to the housing complex, all of our clothes and belongings are packed, but Musa calls everyone into a meeting in the middle of the courtyard of the housing complex. Musa asks Qasa, how much gold is left. Qasa informs Musa that only ten camels worth of gold has been used. Musa orders twenty-five camels' worth of gold be readied for distribution. With each camel carrying three hundred pounds each, that is over 7,000 pounds of gold.

Qasa says that if Musa is planning on distributing this much gold, the price of gold in Egypt would crash. Musa tells Qasa that is an issue Al-Nasir will have to handle, but the people of Egypt will be happy. Musa demands that every diplomat, prince, merchant, and counselor also be sent gold. Musa tells me to make sure the statue that he broke in the church is replaced.

"I know you wish to attend Hajj this year, but I need you to travel back to Gao," Musa tells Segaman. "I want you to camp outside of the walls of Gao, nothing comes in and nothing leaves. Give the women and children a chance to leave, and have them escorted to Djenne."

Sulayman, clears his throat nervously, "Shall I, begin planning a Council Meeting for when we return?"

"What council? I am the council," Musa says sternly. Musa and Sulayman exchange glances. With his eyes, Musa tells Sulayman he knows everything. Slaves quickly move about sending gold to the palace, I make sure Al-Jashnakir receives an amount worthy of our partnership. As we leave Cairo, we toss gold to people cheering and waving, "Musa! Musa!" the growing crowd shouts as we give gold to the old and young, Muslims and non Muslims. There was not a person in Cairo who did not enjoy the gold of Mansa Musa.

As night fell and we set up camp, the conversation on everyone's tongue was the events in Cairo and the excitement of Mecca. The excitement of Mecca came and went, the highlight of Mecca was Musa meeting an architect from Granada, Abu Ishaq as-Shaili, who Musa persuaded to return back to the empire and work for him to build, a city of gold and ink, as Musa has started calling Timbuktu. As we leave Mecca, travel around Cairo, to approach Gao, the mood of the caravan shifts. Many people who travelled with us return to home, the only woman left with us is Fajr, whose love for her brother and husband would not allow her to leave.

Approaching Gao; tents, horses, and camp fires stretch as far as the eye can see. We arrive to the camp to cheers from the soldiers. We are greeted by Segaman and his top commanders. Musa's large tents, equipped with a sleeping cot, a large desk, and chests of clothes sits in the middle of the camp. Segaman explains how the women and children were escorted to Gao under military protection and the only ones left behind the walls was the military of Gao. Musa commands Sulayman to work with Segaman to work on a plan to break the wall of the city if diplomacy fails. "Too many times I failed to follow failed diplomacy with military action. We have the hyena by the tail, and now we shall drive the spear through its neck," Musa says.

DEAR FATHER,

It saddens me to hear the betrayal of Uncle Umar. I am sure you will administer justice based on the laws of the Qur'an and Sunnah of our beloved Prophet. I have sent the desired number of troops to General Segaman and have a large number of standby. Communication lines have been established between Gao and Djenne, messengers are at your command.

In other news, I know you have looked for a marriage for me on your journey. If I may say, there is a new woman at court. Although we have spoken only a little, her beauty and wit is unmatched. I dare say I am in love. Upon your return I would like you and mother to make a proper introduction. I will not tempt myself and keep a safe distance, only admiring her from afar.

-Magha

THE KINGDOM OF GAO
1326

Musa hands me a letter from Magha and I run my eyes over each line. "It would kill him to know two uncles have betrayed this family," Musa says while a slave holds a mirror as he fixes his beard. Musa dismisses the slave and continues. "And apparently the boy is in love, does he not want a proper marriage?"

"You know how his generation is, they want everything the heart desires and they will deal with the repercussions later," I respond. I fold the letter and place it on the desk, "Any news on the talks with Umar?"

Musa sits next to me on the large floor pillow in his tent. "He still refuses to come out, but he also refuses war. If not for Fajr, I would have reduced these walls to a pile of dust already." Musa says pointing to the walls through the tent. "We did not speak much in Mecca, did you enjoy hajj?"

I wish I could tell him the truth. While he and everyone was crying and lifting their hands to Allah, I felt nothing. Seeing the Kaba, throwing stones, and all of the other rituals did not move my heart. When I did cry it was because I was sad for not being able to cry, in fear I was losing my faith. I turn to Musa, and do what I have done many times, lie to him. "It truly lifted my spirits, inshaAllah we get the chance to go again."

After a week of failed diplomacy, demanding Umar to vacate his throne, and no military action, anxiousness fills the camp. As I wander around the camp, some men read, some sharpen their swords and spears, some spend time training their horses. "Ishaq?" I say to a man sitting on a wooden chest.

"Ah, Isa, good to see you again," he says without looking up from his book.

"I thought you had gone to Djenne," I say in curiosity.

Ishaq closes his book. "Not at all, Musa wants me right here," he says knocking on the wooden chest. "I have been designing universities and mosques for Timbuktu, and whatever else Mansa Musa wishes," Ishaq says.

"You're from Granada right? Spain?" I ask. "How is it there?"

"It is, dare I say, an empire in decline. Fountains that once ran with water as blue as the sky are now as dry as the Sahara . Our history is complicated, either we have political stability and a lull in culture or political dysfunction and vibrant culture. There needs to be a balance," he says balancing his book on his index finger.

"Sounds very hectic," I respond.

"Tell me about Timbuktu," he asks with a wide smile.

"In all honesty I have never been. I am certain neither has Mansa Musa."

"Then what awaits us is truly a surprise," he says raising his eyebrows in delight. "You're lucky, you know. Mansa Musa holds you in very high regards."

"Does he?" I say surprisingly. Sometimes it is hard to tell how Musa really feels about someone. Even those of us who have known him our entire lives have a hard time reading him.

"All he did was talk about you and his son, I know more about you than I know about him!" he says laughing. "He is under a lot of stress, his eyes are heavy, but I fear his soul is heavier." Ishaq is interrupted by generals shouting out commands and soldiers running into formations. Ishaq and I sit on the wooden chest as the world around us grows hectic. Musa emerges from his tent, surrounded by his guards. Archers take aim at three horseman carrying a white flag slowly making their way from the walled city towards the camp. Musa mounts his horse and orders his military to stand down.

Musa meets the three men in the empty space between the walls of the city and the camp. One of the men hands Musa a piece of paper, as Musa looks it over he rides back to camp. He enters his tent and within minutes Musa exits the tent then walks to Fajr's tent, which is equal in luxury and size. Both of them make the slow walk towards me.

"Umar wants to meet with Fajr and I want you to escort her inside," Musa tells me as Fajr stands silently. I do as I am told without protest as Fajr and I enter Gao, which is nothing more than an empty shell. The life that had once lived here has found a new shell. We are escorted into the palace, through a maze of halls and into the throne room. Not a person in sight as we enter, only a rancid smell that forces Fajr and I to cover our noses. Umar, sits on his throne, a sword dangling from his hand.

"Brother," she says as she approaches the throne holding out her hand commanding me to stay behind her.

"Sister," Umar says in a raspy voice.

"When is the last time you bathed?" Fajr asks as she sits on the floor next to the throne.

"Three weeks, maybe four, your husband's army has halted water from coming inside the gates. Bathing is now a luxury in Gao." Fajr

93

slowly tries to take the sword, but Umar moves it to his other hand. "Remember when we were kids? And father would tell us stories of great rulers of Gao?" Fajr, who I have never seen cry, not even when Musa returned from Taghaza riddled with arrow scars began to cry and she nodded her head, silently saying yes I remember. "I wanted to be one of them," Umar also begins to cry. A part of me wonders if I should be in the room as they share this intimate moment.

"Why did you do it? Do you know how much danger you put me in!" Fajr bellows as her voice bounces off of the walls of the room. Umar sits on his throne, silent, seemingly unbothered by his sister's tears. There is a certain distant gloss in his eyes, as if he is trying to look into his future or relive his mistakes. He stares off into the room as if he is reliving the very moment that put him in this situation, wondering what he would do different to avoid this very situation.

"Is he going to kill me?" Umar asks. Fajr with a face full of tears finds humor in his question, or maybe a bit of sadness forced her to laugh to keep from crying more. Umar places the tip of the sword to his throat. "If you love me, push this through my neck. I would rather die on my throne still a king," he says.

Fajr stands up and takes the sword, they pass whispers between themselves, Fajr lifts the sword and slowly passes it through Umar's throat as she recites prayers, crying the entire time. She drops the sword as Umar slumps in his throne, struggling to breathe, with each breath he inches closer to death. "Bring Musa here," she commands me. When I return with Musa, Fajr is once again holding the sword with no evidence that she was sobbing.

"What did you do?" Musa asks, approaching with caution. Fajr throws the sword at Musa's feet as the sound of metal hitting the floor echoes throughout the room.

"I did what you would have had others do for you," she says. "My nephews have fled. You know what that means Musa?" she asks. "I am the legitimate ruler of Gao. I am the sole heir to this throne," she says pointing at the throne, ignoring her brother who is slumped over.

"You killed your brother?" Musa asks, narrowing his eyes trying to believe the sight before him.

"That is secondary, the fact is Gao is mine and I want to govern it as my father would have," she says. Musa, still in disbelief gazes at Umar's lifeless body on the throne, no doubt thinking of his own immortality. A living king gazing up the body of a deceased king.

"You and I both know, that cannot happen," Musa says to her. "Did you really think that was a possibility? Is that why you slit his throat! Because you wanted to rule?" Fajr, raises her arms as if to say, of course, is that not why you kill? "There are political realities that we cannot change Fajr!"

"That, that right there, that is it. You do not see that you create political realities," she says pointing at Musa. "We are all here because of a political fantasy you wanted to make a reality. Cairo, Mecca, Gao, and soon Timbuktu, all fantasies that you, Musa, made realities. You are not as helpless as you make people to believe," she says turning her back to him.

Musa massages his temples with his thumb and index finger. "You can choose the administration, make all the treaties, even live here for all I care. The world needs to think that I killed Umar," Musa says. Fajr turns to Musa and bows and he bows to Fajr. As I gaze upon the spectacle of Musa and Fajr, I wonder how they coexisted for so long? How can such unchecked ambition live under one roof? Maybe, this is why they refuse to share a tent and maybe the roof of the palace is just an illusion for them. This cannot be the first time they discussed this, but I am sure it is last time they will discuss this. Fajr outsmarted Musa.

Musa walks over to Umar's body and smears blood on his arms and face, picks up the sword as the three of us stroll back to the camp. As we approach, and the soldiers see a bloody Musa carrying a sword, they cheer and clap. Spears dance in the air as Musa, Fajr, and I move through the crowd. As soldiers pat me on the back as if I helped, I pray for the rest of my life, I see no more murder. I have seen more people killed in these past months than in my entire life. When we enter Musa's tent, he tells Segaman to send a letter to Jarrah.

"Gao has fallen into my hands as Umar fell under my blade. My army will be at the walls of Timbuktu in the coming weeks. For the sake of the Muslims that you have oppressed in your kingdom, your rule has come to an end," Musa says as Segaman writes.

"Go retrieve Umar's body, give him a burial fit for a Muslim and a king. On to Timbuktu," Musa says while cleaning blood off of his hands with a damp cloth given to him by a slave.

THE KINGDOM OF TIMBUKTU 1326

"Where did I put that those plans?" Ishaq says while fumbling with his collection of architecture plans. I ask for which university and he replies, Djinguerber. When we arrived in Timbuktu, King Jarrah had already fled the city. No doubt fearful of meeting the same fate as Umar. Musa immediately put Ishaq to work constructing and repairing buildings, including the masjid that was destroyed by Jarrah. "Found it!" he shouts as he holds his drawings up to the sunlight.

"I like the idea of steps on the outside that lead inside," I chime in while looking over his shoulder. Without turning to me, Ishaq nods in agreement. Ishaq shouts orders to workers as they do his bidding. Ishaq tells me to walk with him, as we venture around the city under the hot morning sun. We approach an empty plot of land and he tells me this is where the girls school will go.

"Sologon University," Ishaq leans in and tells me. "Named after the mother of Keita clan, I do believe."

"Yes, she was the mother of Sundiata, who was the founder of the Mali Empire," I say.

Ishaq shrugs his shoulders. "Never heard of him," he replies.

"Salaam-al-laykum," a voice says. When I turn around a tall young man dressed in Tuareg fashion is standing behind us.

"Wa-laykum-as-salaam," I say while Ishaq takes his leave, assuming that the young man and I were friends who needed some privacy.

"Isa? Correct?" I nod my head and the young man introduces himself as Yaya, a young kola nut merchant who was born and raised in Timbuktu.

"What can I help you with?" I ask.

"I wrote to Mahga weeks ago about this issue, but I have heard no response. He has been here many times laying the ground work for many projects and he is the only one I know who I could talk to," Yaya's hands begin to shake and his voice starts trembling.

"How did you find me?" I ask

"I asked who was in charge and everyone kept pointing to you, so I followed you until I felt safe to tell you. Until you were somewhat alone," he says.

I motion for him to keep talking. "Not everyone is happy with Musa's annexation of Timbuktu, especially the merchants. They may plan a rebellion," he blurts out. My first instinct is to look around us to see if anyone overheard us, but we are all alone.

"Who are these merchants?" Yaya begins to speak but I cut him off. "Gather all of them together. Tell them to meet me right here after Ishaa."

Torches in the distance begin to make their way to the future site of Sologon University as I stand in the empty plot of land. I introduce myself to everyone and ask what issues they have. I regret the decision instantly. The group yells at me all at once, a young man seems irate as he insults my mother.

"Kawsu!" Yaya yells, trying to cool tensions.

"We have all heard the stories of Mansa Musa. He enslaves who he wants, he takes land when he wills, he does what he wants! And now he wants to tax us only to further his riches?" Kawsu says pointing at his chest.

It is very hard to argue with the truth because that is exactly what Musa wants to do. "We all know he wants Timbuktu so he can control the trade going to North Africa," another man says.

"Exactly!" Kawsu replies.

I wait for them to quite down. "Brothers, I promise you there will be no new taxes on any goods."

Kawsu laughs at my statement. "And how can we take your word? Who are you to make such a promise?"

"We want a meeting with Mansa Musa himself!" another man shouts. I hate to say that at this very moment Musa is somewhere in Timbuktu but I am unsure as to where. I tell the rambunctious crowd I will talk to Musa and set up a meeting as soon as I can. As the men begin to disperse into the night, I call Yaya over to me.

"I need you to stay by my side," I tell him.

After days of working with Ishaq and not seeing Musa I set out to find him where I assume he would be, Jarrah's old palace. Although, it is not the same size as the palace in Djenne, it has many of the same features. When I enter, slaves are busy working, bringing the palace up to the standards of Musa. As I roam the hallways going unnoticed by those occupying space I spot Musa sitting on a bench that is placed in a hallway, all alone. He is looking out of a window, aimlessly gazing. It feels almost criminal to disrupt a person when they look this peaceful. Over the years, I have rarely seen Musa alone or peaceful, he is always running to a meeting or surrounded by people.

"You found me," he says as I stand in the hallway with my hands behind my back, waiting to be seen.

"Were you hiding?" I ask as he motions me to look out of the window with him. As I gaze out of the window, merchants are busy selling, wagons pulled by camels enter and exit my frame of vision, a flock of birds takes flight, soaring to their destination.

"I have been hiding. Fajr went back to Djenne, you have been with Ishaq, I have not been alone for this long my entire life," he says as we both laugh at the sad truth. My smile disappears and Musa senses that I have bad news. "What is it?" he asks.

"The merchants, they want a meeting with you. They are ready to rebel if you impose new taxes on their goods," I say regrettably.

Musa stands and turns his back to the window. "Why people think they can delay the inevitable is beyond me," he says. "What did you tell them?"

I explain how I met with them after a young merchant named Yaya sought me out. I met with them and told them there will be no new taxes, but they were eager to meet him. "Bring them here tomorrow. I will...," Musa trails off as he gazes out the window. "I will settle their fears."

As I leave, Musa calls my name. "I still have no desire to know how you came into possession of those letters. But do tell me this," he says as I sit back down. "Whatever you had to do, or whatever you have been doing. Has it been hard on you?" he asks while turning his body towards me.

"These few years," I say as I feel a rush of honesty sprout from my tongue, "have been hard, but everything I have done was for the betterment of the empire."

"And yourself," Musa says slicing through my failed attempt at humility.

"Where is Sulayman?" I finally ask.

"Here in the palace, heavily guarded," he says while walking down the hallway.

The next day, merchants, far more than at the meeting I had arranged stream into the palace. Soldiers, line the hallways as the merchants are shown into the throne room of the palace. Not as opulent as the throne room Musa is accustomed to, but still a sight to see. Musa has transformed himself from humble servant wearing white to a king of kings, covered in purple linen and gold jewelry.

Yaya finds standing room next to me as we gaze on the group of merchants together from a wall. With Kawsu as their spokesman, he tells Musa of their fears of high taxation, religious oppressions on non-Muslims, and overall tyranny. Musa sits regally on his throne as he overlooks the audience. He sits on his throne surveying the crowd as silence and anticipation looms in the air.

"I can make three promises," Musa says sitting on his throne. "No non Muslim will be forced to convert to Islam. Like in all corners of my empire, non-Muslims are welcome and will be protected just as Muslims. You will not pay jizya nor be forced to serve in the military." The merchants nod and smile at the news. He is off to a great start.

"Promise number two; no new taxes will be imposed on your goods. I will be fair in all economic dealings." The merchants who were once skeptical begin to applaud Musa. "Promise number three; I will slaughter anyone who rebels against my rule." The applause stops, as suddenly the soldiers holding their swords and spears in resting position, unsheathe their weapons. Musa stands from his throne and approaches Kawsu. "Do we have terms," he says while extending his arm.

Kawsu, satisfied or terrified, maybe both, shakes Musa's hand. With the shake of a hand, Musa, as he promised during Ramadan, took Timbuktu without a single drop of blood being shed. Although he was more than willing to spill however much it took.

Under the unforgiving sweltering sun that shines on slaves and kings alike, we make out way back to Djenne. Musa calls for water as a slave on a camel gallops to him with a water container. Musa hands me the container and I take a couple of sips. Musa tells the slave to make sure the others stay hydrated as well. "When we get home," Musa says while petting his camel. "Draw up papers for a tax increase on goods in Timbuktu within six months. Also, increase the military presence on all trade routes within four months," I reply with a nod. Musa turns to me and stops his camel. "I will not be dictated to by my subjects," he says while playing with a ruby ring on his finger.

DJENNE, MALI 1327

Musa took my advice and left Kawsu to govern Timbuktu, all he has to do is collect the proper taxes and Kawsu will live like a king. Fajr has secretly been governing Gao, placing a puppet king on the throne, a distant cousin who can be controlled and manipulated at will.

Returning to Dejenne after almost two years of traveling is bitter but sweet. I wish I could see more of this vast world, but I have missed home. I missed Aminta, the boys, the palace, the food, I missed everything. Not seeing Magha for two years, I have realized how old we have all gotten. Time is neither friend or enemy, but a passive aggressive force which cannot not be controlled or denied.

"We are going to be late!" Aminta says as we rush to the palace. Today is the day Magha introduces his mystery lover to Fajr, Musa, and the entire Malian court. The audience hall is full, but our seats on the balcony overlooking the hall, are reserved as usual. As drummers drum the beat of festivities, Magha is below us, talking and laughing with his contemporaries. Musa grabs Fajr's hand and kisses it. All of their dreams have come true. Timbuktu and Gao are in their pockets. Musa has also destroyed the gold economy in Egypt with his generosity. Sulayman is free, but Musa has someone following him at all times. Ishaq is working on their behalf to create buildings hat will stand for generations, including renovations of the palace. History will remember this as Musa's height of power.

"Father," Magha says as the drumming stops. "Mother," Magha says, bowing to both of them. "Allow me to introduce, Samira," he says as I inch towards the edge of my chair. The curly hair browed skinned girl that I sent to the palace as a slave is now decorated in jewels and fine clothes. My jaw hangs open as I cannot look away from her transformation. She introduces herself as a lowly midwife, who has been searching for work.

"You're not from noble birth?" Musa asks. Samira shakes her head and says Allah did not bless her with high birth.

"Welcome to court Samira, we shall talk marriage!" Fajr says as the drums continue and the sound of clapping fills the hall. Samaria and I make eye contact as she slowly bows her head to me.

Aminta taps Fajr, "Amazing! We would love to have her over for a nice meal tonight!" she yells over the drumming and clapping. I have not left the edge of my seat as I still cannot take my eyes off of Samira.

When we finally make our way back home, I tell Aminta everything. How we went to Egypt, killed Girando, found her, sent her here, and now she is possibly going to be the next Queen of Mali.

Aminta laughs a deep hardy laugh. "Well, good for her," she says dismissing my worries.

"What do you mean good for her? This could be the end of everything if Musa finds out!" I have never shouted at Aminta before and she seems to be totally unbothered by my furious tone.

"Calm down," she says. "Talk to her and see what she has to say. Personally, I like her, I may not know her but I like her." I sit on the floor watching Aminta bring food inside for our meal. In my mind, I have the image of Musa calling for my death because his son fell in love with a slave, a slave in which I personally had escorted to the palace, but not before I killed one of his business partners.

A knock at the door evaporated the scenes of my decapitation. Samira enters and complements the lovely smell of the stew. "Stop sulking on the floor and greet our guest," Aminta says.

"I am sorry, butthere is no way you can do this," I say while shaking my head.

"Do what?" Samira says, shifting her weight to one leg to another. Her hair, loosely covered with a hijab, exposing bundles of her hair.

"This!" I say pointing to her silk scarf, jewels, and overall being. "There is no doubt Magha loves you, but that love will fade once you are gone. I will pay for you to live anywhere else but here," I say.

Aminta disregards my plea and escorts Samira over to the large floor pillows to enjoy the stew while it is still hot. The two, as if I am not in the room, begin to eat, and my anger of being ignored consumes me. "Either you leave! Or I tell Musa the truth!" I say while standing by the door.

Samira takes a sip of the soup. "That would be a bad idea, Isa. Because, you see, there is information that I have that is very valuable to you," she says without looking at me. Still standing by the door I grow silent.

"Sit down," Aminta says to me patting an empty space on the floor.

"I know you want the truth Isa. I can only imagine the confusion that entered your heart when the slave you saw in Egypt appeared before you. But the story goes deeper, I have been sold many times over. Never again will I be sold," she says. There is a certain intensity in her eyes that I have only seen in one other person, Musa. "As I have been sold from harem to harem I have spent time in Morocco, serving in the court of Utham. As I open my legs to men, they would open their mouths around me, usually not knowing I was listening. But it is his son, Ali that you have to worry about," she says breaking off a piece of bread and eating it.

"Worry about? How so?" I ask.

"Emir Ali, Sultan Uthman's son, is very ambitions. His father, may not want to expand the empire as much as his son plans to. Part of Ali's plan, is Timbuktu, which Musa just recently came in possession of."

I look at Aminta who raises her eyebrows as if to say, I told you to hear her out. I burry my face in my hand. I had lost my appetite before dinner started, but now I am afraid I will never be able to eat again.

"So what do we do?" Aminta asks. Samira shrugs her shoulders.

"Do you still want me to leave?" Samira asks. I tell her she has proven herself useful, but under no circumstances is anyone, not even Fajr, to know of her past. For all they know, her parents died, and she began to travel from empire to empire as a midwife. As the night creeps in, I tell Aminta that the best plan would be to have Magha and Ali meet face to face. There are no strong diplomatic ties between us, but that is more reason than ever to establish them. Just when I thought the threats had subsided, the vultures have begun to circle.

A proud Musa and Fajr celebrate with the new bride and groom, along with the rest of the empire in celebrating the marriage of Samira and Magha. Samira, with no family, asked me to be her wali, in which I gladly accepted. As I walk around the last day of celebration, Ishaq, who has come from Timbuktu for the festivities, draws pictures of animals for children, vendors peddled their goods, even Sulayman with Qasa and his wife Aza made an appearance.

It has been over two months since we have returned from Timbuktu and I replay the night that Samira told me of Emir Ali in my mind over and over. At such a young age, she knew how to use information to her advantage. The day she asked me to be her wali she confessed she never wanted to put me in an awkward position. She looked me in my eyes and told me she would to anything to never have to beg for food again. When she came to Dejnne, she had no evil intentions, but the opportunity to fall in love with a prince was presented to her and she took it. I not only understand why she did it, but I am envious of her ability to take control of her own life.

The palace is empty on the last night of the wedding festivities as Samira and I walk the halls of the palace. We talk about her time in Morocco and about my time as a fisherman. I tell her about the issues between Sulayman and I and the plan to replace him in the succession. "Have you even been on the balcony of the audience hall?" I ask. She shakes her head no and I take her up the narrow and dimly lit stairwell. As we step on to the balcony, Sulayman is bellow us, sitting at a table surrounded by guards. I am reminded of myself, years ago, sitting at a table surrounded by guards, looking up at Musa, Abu Bakr, and Sulayman. Then, I did not know I was witnessing an event that would change not only the empire, but the entire course of history. This time, I am looking down from the shadows of the balcony. Musa enters the hall dragging a sword behind him, the sound of steel trailing him. He commands the guards to leave, leaving only Musa and Sulayman below us.

"Well, brother, is this what you were waiting for? To execute me in an empty room?" Sulayman says while trying to contain his nervous laughter.

"I read the letters between you and Girandino. You were feeding him information and he was feeding information to Umar," Musa says while moving the blade from the floor to Sulayman's neck.

Sulayman narrows his eyes as if he is confused at the allegations levied against him. "Is that what all is about?" he says softly. "The guards, the isolation, the sword," he says pointing to the blade. "Because you think I tried to kill you?"

"Did you or did you not tell Girandino my every move! Were you not feeding him information? Yes, or no, Sulayman!" Sulayman nods his head. Samira tugs on my arm saying we should go before they see us but I shush her.

"I had no idea what he was doing with the information, I swear. I was simply sharing court gossip."

"That is not just gossip, you are much smarter than that, Sulayman. You were giving out military plans. To a European at that!" Musa yells, his voice bouncing off the walls.

Sulayman points to Musa's sword. "Are you going set the world right by killing me? Like you have killed many before me that have stood in your way? No doubt, brother, the world will remember you as a great and generous ruler. The man who gave away the worlds weight in gold, liberated Timbuktu, and prayed five times daily. We both know the truth."

Musa's arm begins to shake as he tries to hold back tears, sniffling and blinking rapidly. "They will probably say, 'Mansa Musa built a new masjid every Friday.'

You would like that?" Sulayman steps away from Musa's blade.

Musa throws down the sword, and grabs a fist full of Sulayman's clothing. "You will publicly relinquish your claim to the throne! The throne and the empire will be passed down to Magha and his heirs! Not you and your idiot of a son! Now leave!" Sulayman, as instructed leaves Musa, who exhales deeply picking up his sword and leaves out of a different door. Samira walks over to the throne, and just as Musa did years ago, she runs her hands over the ivory armrest.

"It seems your plan actually worked," she says while making herself comfortable on the throne.

SALAAMS PRINCE MAGHA,

I have received your invitation to visit Dejenne and I humbly accept.
The disposing of your uncle as heir and your inevitable accession
brings me great pleasure. The tales of your bravery, especially
dealing with the rebels are well known here in Fes. Building an
alliance between our future empires is one of the greatest goals I
seek to accomplish before I take the throne. I look forward to
meeting you, until then, as a brother in Islam and fellow Prince, I
wish you nothing but blessings from Allah.

-Emir Ali

DJENNE, MALI 1337

The weeks after news broke that Magha was heir to the Mali Empire were not as hectic as I thought they would be. Magha, although he did not know it, was molded to be Mansa. Nobody has been happier than Fajr, who effectively controlled Gao, and now had the ear of the current and future Mansa.

Sulayman officially relinquished all claim to the throne of Mali, citing that he would much rather end his days focusing on Islamic studies and menial government tasks. More importantly, to avoid Emir Ali from plundering Timbuktu, Samira persuaded Magha to invite Emir Ali to Djenne on an official state visit. Magha ordered for Ishaq to complete renovations and improvements to the palace before Ali's visit, no detail was left unattended to. Walls were cleaned, new drums were carved, and new clothes for the royal family were made.

Moroccan oud players and Malian drummers filled the refurbished dining hall with a lovely mix of Fez and Djenne music. Local food and traditional Moroccan food flooded the dining hall being carried to tables occupied by ambassadors, diplomats, and wealthy merchants.

"So young," Aminta leans in and whispers to me as she places a handful of rice in her mouth. Musa and Fajr watch over the party on their raised platform, but tonight belongs to the next generation. Those of us who have been blessed by the graces of Musa over the past few years have been banished to tables, watching the young people enjoy themselves. Joining us at our table are the advisors that Ali's father, Sultan Uthman sent with him. The Malian women show the Moroccan women local dances and when the oud players take the lead the Moroccan women show the Malian women their dances. Samira, has already mastered a few of our dances and seems to glide

111

on the floor, swaying her hips to the drums and strings. Ali's wife, Fatima looks on cautiously, but is dragged onto the floor by Samira.

"His mother, she is Abyssinian," a clean shaven Moroccan man with deep wrinkles says to me from across the table.

"I can see, he is rather, dark," I reply over the drums.

"They call him the 'Black Emir' back home," he says. "Muhammad al-Wahid," the man says while extending his hand to me over the table. I shake his hand and introduce him to Aminta. He tells me he is Sultan Uthman's top advisor and was sent to make sure Ali stays out of trouble. In return I explain my duties here in Dejenne as Musa's chief of council. As I am talking I notice that Muhammad is distracted.

"Are you unwell?" I ask.

"No, I apologize for my rudeness, for some reasons I feel as though I have seen Princess Samira before," he says while pointing at Samira who is sharing a story with some young Moroccan and Malian men. Aminta pinches my leg under the table.

"Muhammad, let me show you the courtyard and stables. Maybe some fresh air will clear your head a bit," I say while standing up, leaving him little room to decline my offer. If he recognizes Samira who knows what will happen next. I lead him to the courtyard as the sun dips below the horizon, signaling the coming of Maghrib. I show Muhammad some of our horses, explaining our military training tactics which I hear Segaman talking about from time to time.

"Enough small talk," Muhammad says as I motion for the stable boy to leave. "We are worried about the new regime Musa is allowing to succeed him. As excited as Ali is for an ally outside of Morocco, we have certain agreements with Sulayman. No offense, but your Prince has no idea how to govern and I fear he will surround himself with people just as clueless as himself."

I brush invisible dust off of Muhammad's shoulder. "You have no need to worry. I and the rest of Musa's advisors are going to ensure he is ready when his time comes. We may be old, but we are not dead," I say laughing

"Samira," Muhammad says while looking at one of the horses curiously. "She has such a familiar face. I feel as though I have encountered her somewhere before," he says while he brushes the horse with his hand.

"She truly is a child of the world. I felt the same way when I first encountered her," I say trying to lead him away from his current train of thought. "She has a love for gold."

"Speaking of gold," Muhammad says, "the stunt that Musa pulled in Egypt, it was a stunt was it not?"

I invite Muhammad into the courtyard, so we can talk and make sure nobody is around us. Hiding in the open rather than lurking in the dark stables. "Musa was feeling very generous, basically overcome with the spirit of Hajj. I promise you it was no stunt," I say while gazing at the disappearing sun.

"Right," Muhammad says, exhaling deeply at my reply. "Well, thank you for the brief tour, I shall find my way to my room, it is getting late," Muhammad says while ending with a bow. "Tomorrow you should show me this famous library I keep hearing about," he says while walking away.

I make my way back to the dinning hall where the party has no sign of ending. Musa and Fajr made their way from the raised platform to the table where the older people have been banished to.

"I think this is the first time you two have been in a room and have been ignored," I say to Musa and Fajr as I take my seat next to Aminta, kissing her hand. Fajr waves her hand in the air, dismissing my joke while Musa laughs.

"Wait, wait, wait," Ali says as the music stops and the dining hall grows silent. "We need to acknowledge the real hosts of this evening, Mansa Musa and Muso Mansa Fajr! Your hospitality is much appreciated! May your reign continue to be prosperous, insha'Allah."

Musa and Fajr, stand as the dining hall erupts in applause, someone yells out "The Liberator of Timbuktu!" which brings a huge smile over the face of Musa.

"Your visit here is most welcome. Fajr and I will retire now, but do not allow our absence to end the festivities. Eat, dance, and enjoy this very rare of occasions!" Musa says while Fajr stands and locks her arm with Musa. After two more songs, Aminta and I drag ourselves back to the house.

"Muhammad? He recognized Samira?" she asks while applying Egyptian skin cream to her face.

"He did and he asked again when we stepped outside. I changed the conversation to gold. He knows something or he will remember something very soon," I reply. Aminta turns to me and purses her lips as if to say, do something and do it quick.

The call to prayer is forced from the lungs of the muezzin as he tries to stretch his voice to all the houses in the area. Without much sleep I drag myself out of bed and walk to the masjid. There is a cool breeze in the causing sand to dance in the air. I kick off my sandals as a slave outside the entrance grabs a bucket of water collected from

114

the Bani River. I give salaams to people as they pass as I lean against the wall as another gust of wind pushes sand towards us. I pour water over my hands, feet, arms, and face.

I wipe water from my face with my sleeve and begin to walk up the steps to enter the masjid. When I enter I see Ali and Magha sitting next to each other. Everything in me wants to avoid them but everything in me wants to walk over to them. I settle on taking a seat behind them. I give salaams as the imam gives the iqama and salah begins. After salaah I gather myself from the floor of the masjid, with a sharp pain in my knee, a sign of old age. Magha and Ali do not miss a beat in helping me to my feet.

"The walk here was fine, but if I sit for too long, the pain is not too far," I say jokingly.

"Well, we are glad you walked over, we were just talking about you," Magha says as Ali nods his head as his curly hair jumps up and down. As we walk towards the palace entrance Ali and Magha take turns in explaining how they want to sign an agreement for trade, military, and diplomacy agreement.

"My advisors, well, really my father's advisors have always eyed Timbuktu," Ali says as we reach the palace. "When Mansa Musa annexed it, concerns grew that Mansa Musa was becoming too powerful and talk of war began. The short time I have been here has shown me war is unrealistic and all sides will eventually lose. As progressive as I may be, Muhammad needs to be convinced."

Magha turns to me and grabs me by my shoulders. "Which is where you come in, he needs to be convinced that a relationship between us is positive and that war is negative," Magha interlocks his fingers as Ali once again nods in agreement.

"When I take the throne I know I will be surrounded by enemies, most of whom will be living in the palace. I do not need a war, especially one with a Muslim brother on my plate," Ali says.

"Of course, I applauded you two for choosing peace over war. Tell Muhammad to meet me here in the palace after Maghrib I will have a plan by then."

"I honestly have no idea who he is," Samira tells me as I pace back and forth at home, trying to conceive a plan for dealing with Muhammad in a few short hours. I have come too far to have my head cut from my body if Musa finds out the truth, not only about Samira, but the entire plot to put Magha on the throne.

"What if I go with you?" Samaria suggests. I wave off her suggestion as too risky and continue to pace. "Listen, I do not want this getting out any more than you do," she pleads.

"So you propose I put you two in the same room?"

Samira, gives me a look of determination, stands up, and inhales deeply expanding her chest. "I have seen the worst that this life has to offer, so have you, I have seen the best that life has to offer, just like you. Our fates are intertwined, if you want to believe it or not is up to you, but I need you to trust me on this."

She is right, I do not want to believe that our fates are in the hands of an old man with a bad memory and that we are forever intertwined with a secret that can destroy us both. "Fine, I trust you." She lets out a sigh of relief and wraps her arms around me, hugging me like a daughter hugs her father after finally allowing her a new toy. Aminta and I never had children and at our age, probably never will. I have no desire to take a second wife. The closest I have to feeling the joys of fatherhood is the time I have spent with Samira. I pray my affection for her is not naïve. Everything I have, once again, could come crumbling down like an abandoned termite colony.

As the masjid on the palace grounds empties after Magrhib prayer, I roam the palace, almost aimlessly heading towards my office. I pass a room of generals huddled over a table with maps scattered everywhere. When I enter my office, Muhammad is already there, peering out of the window enjoying the view of the market in the distance.

"Salaam al-laykum," I say, but he is unresponsive. After a few moments of awkward silence and of me standing behind him I try again, "Salaam al-laykum," I repeat.

"I was told your people had very little in the way of modernization. But I look over your markets and I see ironworkers, booksellers, and almost anything one can wish to buy," he says. Suddenly I wish he kept ignoring me.

"We do have a very modern economy," I reply slightly offended but fully proud.

"How is the economy in Timbuktu?" he asks with a smirk. I return his smirk with a smirk of my own, enjoying the battle of wits that is about to take place. A few years ago his passive aggressiveness would have been mistaken for genuine curiosity.

"Did Ali not tell you? He and Magha want peace, which means Timbuktu stays within the fold of the Mali Empire," I say.

"Prince Ali will not stay within the fold of life for too long if he keeps up this charade," Muhammad says folding his arms inching closer to me, trying to intimidate me.

"We are both old men," I say while taking a seat at my desk. "Why are you determined on war? War always impacts the next generation

117

more than the current one. Be reasonable and allow Ali and Magha to shape their future empires the way they wish," I plead trying to appeal to his reasonable side. As soon as he opens his mouth to speak there is a knock on the door. I walk over and open the door and Samira, escorted by two guards, strolls in to the room.

"Salaam al-laykum," she says as she looks between Muhammad and I. Muhammad scoffs while taking a long look at her. "I will keep this brief. I am here under my own will, to plead for you to come to reason," she says looking at Muhammad. "Outside of the palace walls there are four carts full of gold. You can leave right now and go anywhere in the world you want. Or stay here and cause trouble, trouble that will eventually lead to your downfall if you live that long," she says while standing as still as a wood carving.

Muhammad's eyebrows fall inward. "Do you think I will be negotiated to by a woman!" he bellows. He fails to understand this in not a negotiation, he has no say in the terms of the deal.

"Men and their pride," she says while sighing. "What difference does it make who is offering you the deal? Fine, Isa, repeat what I just said if that would make our guest more comfortable." I look at Muhammad without saying a word, the room grows silent. "The deal is off," she says abruptly.

"Wait!" Muhammad screams, loud enough for the entire empire to hear him. "I accept," he says.

Samira opens the door and is handed a piece of paper. "Copy this letter in your own handwriting sign it and leave it in your room. You will leave by tomorrow morning." He looks over the letter and hangs his head in shame. I offer him my desk as he sits and copies the letter and signs it. He hands me the paper and slowly walks towards the door refusing eye contact with Samira.

"Where are you from?" he finally asks. "You have such a familiar face."

Samira opens the door and silently commands Muhammad to leave. She closes the door behind him then runs into my arms. I kiss her on the forehead and hand her the letter.

The next morning in the courtyard Musa asks Ali what the letter says. Ali explains how Muhammad wanted to live the rest of his life in the City of the Prophet and has removed himself from politics. He urges Magha and Ali to always chose peace over war, especially when glory and gold is involved. He regrets that he did not have a chance to say goodbye to everyone in Fes, but he has to follow his heart.

"You have to respect his commitment to Islam," Musa says hanging his head low in what seems to be reflective thinking. Magha kicks a pebble across the courtyard floor sending it skipping and tumbling. He reminds us at least now the peace deal can go through largely interrupted. "My son," Musa says patting Magha on the back, "always the positive thinker."

Rapid footsteps turn the corner and Segaman approaches us, he quickly bows and asks if it is appropriate to speak freely, giving Ali a look of general mistrust. Musa answers by saying we are all family and there are no secrets between family. Segaman, still apprehensive of the presence of Ali is urged by Magha to speak.

"Very well," Segaman says. "The merchants in Timbuktu are in rebellion, masjids are being torn down, tax collectors are being sent away or kidnapped, libraries are being burned." Musa sucks his teeth.

"I told them, I told them if they rebel against my rule, there will be consequences," Musa says in a solemn voice. Years ago he would have yelled, grabbed, and slapped.

"I will personally see an end to this rebellion," Magha interrupts. "Even if I have to put every merchant to death!" Magha yells with his nostrils enlarged with rage. Ali and Musa try to calm him, but Magha will have none of it. He pushes his father's hand away and commands Segaman to ready the troops. Segaman glances at Musa for confirmation and Musa gives him a slight nod.

Ali, Magha, and Segaman disappear behind the corner exiting the courtyard. Musa places his hand on my shoulder, a hand which once pumped with youth now wrinkled, just like mine. "I need you to go with him. Just to make sure he does not get out of control. I know he feels like he has a lot to prove and may act irrationally." The prospect of trying controlling the prince of the largest gold producing empire is freighting, but what other choice do I have? "This will be the last time, when you return you can retire, I promise," Musa says grinning from ear to ear.

"What of the girl's school?" Aminta asks as I mull over maps and trade agreements from the last six months. "Fajr and I are worried," she continues, but I pay her no mind. "Listen to me!" she demands snatching the paper out of my hand.

"I have listened to you for years!" I howl. "Isa do this better, Isa I want a house, Isa tell me this! All I do is defend us from the outside world and protect this life we have built!" Aminta grabs me by the waist to apologize, but I remove her hands from me. "There will be no girls school," I scoff.

A pounding at the door wakes Fajr and I in the middle of the night as a messenger tells us to come to the palace immediately. We quickly dress ourselves and head to the palace. We enter the same room which Musa was placed when he returned from Tagahza filled with arrow holes, this time his condition is far worse. Musa is laid out on the bed, sweaty and in and out of consciousness. He has the sweating sickness.

The doctors look over him discussing treatment, but everyone in the room knows the outcome. All of us who were here when Musa returned from Tagahza are here again, this time the outcome of Musa's health is far more certain. Magha and Samira enter the room, with every breath Musa takes, Magha grows closer to becoming Mansa Magha of Mali.

Although, Musa lay dying in a pool of his own sweat the world he is soon departing moves on. Taxes must be collected and military plans must be made. Amongst all the organized mayhem, I slip away from the chaos to visit Musa. A doctor is tending to him as I walk in the room. Passing by the guards whose job it is to protect a dying man, I gaze down at an almost lifeless Musa. As I watch his chest struggle to collect air, my throat tightens.

The doctor bows and scurries out of the room. I take Musa's hand and feel the warmth radiating from his body. "Remember when we were kids and you saved me from drowning when the boat we stole tipped over?" I ask knowing he will not answer. "I was swinging my arms trying to instantly learn to swim and you told me to relax." I can feel my throat tighten even more from the tears that are about to come. "I owe you so much," I say sobbing into his hand. "I will do my best to steer Magha into the right direction." I look down at Musa as he continues to struggle to breathe, the end is near, but this is the beginning for so many others. As much as I have tried to make the future certain I stand here uncertain on so much.

Will Magha be a good ruler? Will he ever turn on me? Will Samira's secrets remain secret? Will Morocco and Egypt smell a young ruler and take advantage? Will I actually retire? I let go of Musa's hand carefully place it over his chest. As I leave Musa a feeling comes over me to find Fajr to see if there is anything I can do for her. I roam the palace, and there is an almost festive mood about. The young faces will soon get their chance to prove themselves under Mansa Magha. Young lawyers, scholars, military officers, merchants, have suddenly seen their chance to join the ranks of the elites.

I knock on Fajr's door and after thirty-seconds of waiting a slave allows me into her chambers. Fajr, dressed in all black is aimlessly gazing out of the window, she looks as if she has not slept in days and she probably hasn't.

"We planned for this moment, for Magha to become Mansa," she says half smiling but fully regretful it seems. "We worked behind the scenes for years carefully placing clues in front of Musa to make the right choice." I nod my head in agreement. "Did you think it would come so soon? During so much chaos?" I reply with a silent no. "Sulayman, Qasa, half of the army has vanished," she says.

"I'm sorry?" I say inching towards her asking her to repeat herself.

"They have fled, they could be anywhere hatching any kind of plan," she says. I inhale deeply trying to collect my thoughts. I remind her she has enough on her plate and I will handle Sulayman.

The next morning, the news that everyone has been waiting for came; Mansa Musa has died. Fajr and Magha wash Musa's body and wrap it in white linen. His body is taken to the royal burial site where other his grandfather Abu Bakr II is buried along with other members of the Keita clan. I take a fistful of dirt, whisper "bismillah" and toss it into the grave. I glance over at Magha, who is surrounded by his team of advisors, young men I have never seen or have seen in passing. Samira is by his side as well, along with their guards. He motions me over to him, wraps his arm around me and commands me and Segaman to find Sulayman while he is in Timbuktu dealing with the rebellion. Samira will have full Mansa authority while he is away. I want to tell him I am old and Segaman is older, that this is a job for the young men he has surrounding him, but I bow my head to the new Mansa.

"I will not be the Mansa responsible for the destruction of the Mali Empire," he whispers so only I can hear.

ISA,

I am pleased that you and Segaman have found Qasa, he has successfully arrived in Timbuktu under guard. I urge you to find Sulayman as soon as possible as for any plan he has hatched will be accelerated when he hears of the news of his son. Do not forget that we are operating with half of the army on our side. A civil war is not a situation I want to find myself in. Anything that is within my power to give you in order to come to a swift solution do not hesitate to ask.

-Mansa Magha

NIANI, MALI 1338

"So, even if we do find him, are we supposed to subdue him with half an army when he has the other half on his side? Isa, we have been chasing a ghost for almost three years," Segaman says as he pokes the fire. "Before Musa died he said, the campaign in Timbuktu would be our last big campaign, then he would start delegating matters of state to Magha, slowly of course," he says holding out his hands to signal a slow and steady pace.

"We our old men now and we find ourselves so far from home. I have not seen my wife in years," I say. "For all I know she could be dead." I release a sigh and pull a piece of meat from the bone. "How did you meet Musa?" I ask brazenly.

Segaman laughs. "Through my father, he served Abu Bakr II and like all new rulers you look for the most capable but you do not look too far from the tree that bore you such sweet fruit." I nod my head, realizing even after traveling with Segaman for three years we have never had a real conversation until know.

"You know where we are?" he asks plucking a piece of meat from his teeth. "Niani, the birth place of the empire," he says without giving me a chance to answer.

"Do you ever think of your place in history?" I ask while gazing at the moon. "I have a weird feeling Musa will go down in history, our Hajj journey was no small task," I say laughing.

Segaman chews what meat is on the bone and nods his head in agreement, "Musa solidified his position when he walked through the gates of Gao after he killed Umar, the men, his men, had never seen anything like it."

I look down at the ground as the fire pops, Segaman notices my smile in the light and asks what is so funny. "Musa did not kill Umar, Fajr did." I say while still smiling. "He did not want to commit suicide and he asked her to kill him instead of being humiliated by Musa. So, Fajr ran the blade through her brother, asked me to fetch Musa, then convinced Musa that she had killed him out of cold blood. Umar's body was still warm while Fajr and Musa made a deal to keep the fact she killed Umar silent if she could rule Gao, from the shadows of course. You should have seen Musa's face when he saw Fajr holding that blade."

Segaman holds out his hand, almost like he trying to reach into the fire that separated us. "Are you telling me that Musa did not kill Umar?" I nod my head, plucking a bug for my arm. Segaman lets out a laugh that would shake the stars if possible. "He told all the soldiers this grand story of how he looked Umar in his eyes and said, 'this is for Mali.'" I shake my head

Segaman pours water over his hands. "Even if our names are never told in stories by our children.." he stops. "I am sorry," he says.

"Really, brother no need to apologize. I have come to terms with not having children. Aminta and I have had long conversations about it. Besides, you have much to be proud of, your son will take your position and will be a great general for Magha." Segaman stands up and pats me on the back as he walks back to his tent.

"Tomorrow we continue our travels, we have rested here long enough," he says. A whistling sound rushes over my head as an arrow narrowly misses me, but Segaman falls backwards as an arrow lands in his chest. I turn to run, but I am surrounded by men, Musa's men now under Sulayman's command. Sulayman under the cover of night moves past the men holding a sword in his hand.

126

He slowly walks over to me and once again places his hand around my throat. "You were looking for me while I was following you," Sulayman says as his men surround me. "Allow me tell you how this is going to end; I am going to kill you, march to Timbuktu, save my son, and take the throne that you helped steal from me." A sudden coolness comes over my body as Sulayman plunges the sword through my stomach. The blaze from the fire casts a light on Sulayman and I noticed how much too he has aged. The wrinkles around his eyes have grown as the skin on his neck has started to sag.

He kicks me as I lay on the ground bleeding from my mouth. I turn onto my back as I hear feet scrambling away from the fire. While laying on my back, feeling the blood rushing from my body; I gaze at the stars and recite Al-Fatiah.

DJENNE, MALI 1340

Mari-Dajata walks from his mother over to his grandmother then back to his mother. He leaps into her arms begging to be picked up.

"MashaAllah," Fajr says out of breath, playing with her grandson has tired her. There was a time she could walk the palace grounds all day without losing breath, now tasks such as playing drains her of her energy.

Samira bounces Mari-Djata on her knee as he tries to grab a handful of the neckless that dangles from her neck. "Is there any word of Sulayman and Qasa?" Samira asks batting at the baby who finally grab the necklace.

"After traitors of the army freed Qasa in Timbuktu, the trail as grown cold." There is a knock at the door and Aminta enters carrying a basket filled with silk. She says the buyer never picked up his shipment of silk and does not want it to go to waste. "Will you ever stop working?" Fajr asks while plucking a long piece of purple silk from the basket. Mari-Djata begs for a piece to play with and Aminta hands him a blue piece of silk to twirl around in the air.

Aminta sighs and tries to fight back her tears. She wants to say working helps her keep her mind off of the fact she is a widow, but instead she choses to lie. "Working keeps me young, plus the boys are coming back home soon from Mecca to run the business. I want them to have something to come home to."

Mansa Magha sits at the head of the council table scribbling on a piece of paper as one by one his he receives updates on the empire. Wati, the son of Segaman gives Magha the update on the search for

Sulayman and Qasa. Magha does not look up from his drawing as Wati tells him that over half of the army has now deserted and is more than likely following Sulayman and Qasa planning an attack at any day.

Yaya, a young merchant from Timbuktu who has risen to the ranks of Chief of Council glances at Warti with a concerned look, but words do not pass his lips. "Finished," Magha says looking at his work like a proud father. "A brand new palace," Magha holds up the drawing of a multilevel palace with a large fountain in the courtyard it. Wati and Yaya once again exchange glances as Magha touts his new plans.

That night, as worshippers exit the masjid after Isha prayer, Wati and Yaya walk slower than usual to fit in more words.

"Half of the army…" Yaya says.

"More than half," Wati responds. "Magha is not focused at all, he sits and writes poetry and draws fantasy palaces." Wati stops and places his hand on Yaya's chest. "There is an army, a trained army, with a skilled generals roaming the land and they know where we are. We are literally trapped. They will attack."

Yaya tilts his head to the night sky looking for an answer in the stars.

Yaya remembers the story that Isa told him, the story of how enraged Musa was when Tagahza fell into Egyptian hands. Musa slapped and banished him from court. Yaya has to tell Magha that Bourė, the gold capital of the empire has fallen into rebel hands. A part of Yaya wishes Magha would slap him, banish him, and take charge of the situation like Musa, but he knows that is mere fantasy. When Yaya delivers the news, Magha is sitting with a scribe who is writing the words that leave Magha's mouth. The words are not a letter to a fellow sovereign or an edict, but a poem about the sun.

Magha instructs Yaya to fortify the gold mines that are still within his possession, but Yaya reminds Magha there is not enough men for such a task. Magha, looks at Yaya and says he trusts that he and Wati will create a plan that will save Bouré.

As Yaya sits at his desk, writing letters asking all tribes within the empire to send their able bodied men to Djenne for military training, Samira enters without knocking, with two guards by her side.

"Salaams Yaya," she says. Yaya does not look up from his paper and pen.

"Muso Mansa Samira," he finally stands and bows. "What do I owe this unexpected visit?" Samira glides over to the desk and takes the paper off the desk and reads it to herself.

"You ask these men to serve my husband? Everyone outside these palace walls is tainted, even some in the walls have the smell of rebellion," she says placing the letter back on the desk.

"What would you have me do? The only other option is do to nothing," he replies.

Samira smirks at Yaya's lack of creativity and depth. "Write to Sultan Ali in Morocco. Tell him that his brother in Mali is in need of military assistance."

"Muso Mansa, I feel such requests should come from Mansa Magha, not from you." There is a taste of bitterness in his voice. Resentment that Samira would even dare dictate matters of state.

Samira runs her hands over her silk dress. "My husband spends his days writing poetry and feeding birds. What direction do you think he is able to give?"

Yaya bows and says that he will see to her orders right away. Weeks pass, then months and the letter was not sent. Yaya and Wati recruit men from within the empire, hardened warriors who are veterans of guerrilla warfare, but not well trained in loyalty. The new soldiers are spread thin over trade routes and roads leading into Djenne. They let Sulayman and the rebels move by them without a word, why fight and die for a sovereign who will not fight and die for himself? Overnight Djenne was surrounded by soldiers, soldiers dressed in Malian armor and carrying Malian swords. Sulayman and Qasa sat on their horses, horses protected by heavy quilts. Their flags swayed in the breeze and could be seen from the minerts within the city walls.

The news spread quickly as panic ensued. The panic intensified as Mansa Magha was found lying on the floor, colorless in the face and a cup lying by his side. Dead from poison. No war would be necessary, Sulayman can walk into the gates and sit on the throne with no bloodshed.

Samira finds a slave and tells him to ready the caravan ,her worse fears have come true, but she is fully prepared. She gathers, Mari-Djata, Fajr, and Aminta into a wagon as they sneak out of the city gates.

For an hour the ride is silent, everyone is afraid to speak as the caravan of four trudges along the roads. "Exactly where are we going?" Fajr finally asks.

"My house in Morocco. We will be safe there."

"With what money? We have nothing but the clothes on our backs!" Aminta cries. Samira instructs the caravan to halt as she climbs out and tells the others to follow. She uncovers the first wagon as nuggets of gold shimmer in the sun, wagon number two shines with gold too. Wagon three, clothes, bread, and more gold.

Samira covers the last wagon. "Did you think I was going to entrust my future to a bunch of men? We will be just fine."

SALAAMS PRINCE QASA,

I am more than excited to finally make my way to Djenne as I am only a few days away from the gates of the city. I have rented a house from my cousin in Fez who does dealings in Djenne, Muhammad ibn Faqih. I look forward to the hospitality that I have heard your and your family has bestowed on diplomats, sovereigns, and businessman. May Allah continue to bless you and your father and the people of the Mali Empire.

- Ibn Battuta

DJENNE, MALI 1352

I stand under the silk tent as local judges slowly fill the tent next to me in their wool robes dyed in red. The musicians are playing local songs as the festivities for the famed explorer Ibn Battuta have already started. My father's Chief of Council, Hussain, creeps next to me and tugs at my sword.

"Do you need this for such an occasion," he says pointing at the musicians and silk tent.

"I am still prince of the empire. If I wanted to disarm for important events I would have studied law," I say tugging at his sword-less silk belt. "How was my father this morning," I ask.

"Too tired and weak to move from bed. He has recited prayers all week from bed or a chair," Hussain says softly, not wanting to give any hint of weakness in father. I nod my head at the news when I hear cheering. Ibn Battua's caravan has entered the gates. His skin is light and his beard is heavy, his hair is wrapped in a turban. He embraces me and thanks me for the invitation. We exchange salaams and move form under the sun to the silk tent.

"The journey was long, but I am so glad I am here," he says to me.

"We all have heard of your travels," I say sticking to the script given to me by my father's counselors. "Welcome to *my* kingdom," I say deviating from the planned, "our kingdom." After more small talk I tell him that he is free to go and rest in his rental house. "Tomorrow we feast in your honor," I say while patting him on the back sending him on his way. As we leave a slave hands me a wet cloth and I wipe my hands.

Hussain slows down as if he has something important to tell me. I tell him to speak. "Rohey asks if you would visit her bed tonight." I kiss my teeth and keep walking. She has reduced herself to asking counselors.

"Is everyone gathered? I do not have all day" I ask. Hussain nods his head.

I sit at the head of the council table in the place of my father as one by one, I hear an update on every aspect of the empire. When I do not understand I ask for a better explanation. "Uncle Kanburni, how is our military?" My stepmothers brother has been elevated to general of the army. A small gift for being on the right side of the dispute between Magha and my father.

"All is secure, your majesty, no new news to be told," he says with a smile. I turn to Hussain and he gives me a nod, all business has been completed in the meeting. I stand and out of respect, everyone stands as well. I dismiss myself and flanked by my guards and Hussain move from room to room in the palace conducting business. With the coming of the night I knock on Vida's door. When I open it she is lying on the bed in a silk see-through robe with candles lit, giving the room an orange glow.

"Majesty," she says as she unravels her hair and removes her robe. After we make love she rests her head on my shoulder and I run my finger around her perfectly round breasts. "What is new in your kingdom," she asks full of blissful ignorance. I always love when she asks about politics, for some reason her attempt to access my world is endearing.

"Ibn Battuta is here. I think he is from Fes too," I say.

She perks up. "Yes!" she yells. "I remember when he left for his journey. There was a large celebration for him when he left. I was sold a few weeks later. Now, we both are here under very different circumstances," she says as her voice trails off. I know exactly where she is going with this.

"Have you been denied anything since you arrived here?" I ask her, lifting her chin with me hand. She shakes her head as she plays with the ring encompassing her index finger. I take her face between my hands and kiss her on the forehead. "And you never will." I dress myself and move down the hallway. I stop at Rohey's door and I place my ear against the door. Her snoring prompts me to back away from the door and head back to me chambers.

Bread, meat, fruit, and other foods are brought into the dinning hall as the feast for Ibn Battuta begins. Aaliyah, my father's new wife and sister of Kanburni sits with myself and Rohey on the raised platform. The new dinning hall is roofless and open to the elements, but can be covered with a large tent if needed. Designed by Ishaq, the dinning hall is one of the structures father did not want to destroy in his attempt to eliminate the memory of Musa.

Our food is brought to us as I watch people flock around Ibn Battuta as he regals those around him with his stories of Asia and Europe. Drums start pounding as the attention turns from Ibn Battuta to father as he moves slowly through the crowd. He is using his gold cane as all can see the fragility and wealth of Mansa Sulayman. I help him up the three steps leading the raised platform. A chair is brought up as he takes his seat next to Aaliyah who kisses his hand out of respect. He waves his hand to me and whispers in my ear, his weak chest cannot project loud enough to be heard throughout the hall.

"My father, Mansa Sulayman and Muso Mansa Aaliyah welcome Ibn Battuta and his companions to the Kingdom of Mali! Eat and drink until your bellies are full!" The hall erupts in cheers and applause as people continue the festivities.

Rohey puts her hand on mine underneath the table. Her hand is warm and soft, but I take her hand off of mine and place it on the table. I excuse myself from the table and head towards the courtyard. My guards follow me out the dinning hall as I enter the courtyard. I walk the length of the courtyard, pacing back and forth under the night sky.

I see Hussain out of the corner of my eye as he approaches slowly, unsure if I wanted to be bothered. "Chief of Council," I say, finally acknowledging his existence.

"Majesty," he says then pauses. "Many of the generals wish to call off the search for Samira and her son."

I clasp my hands behind my back as I walk closer to Hussain. Grabbing him by his arm I look him in his eyes. "You tell them to find her and that bastard of her's and do it quickly. Or it will be your head in the end of a spear." I unhand him as he nods his head in agreement.

"Yes, your majesty," he says. I tell him to wait. I know he always means well. Hussain has always been loyal to father and I. He just like many others who were in the military had the choice to join us or Magha. He has proven his loyalty time and time again. He was the messenger who carried letters from father to the European in Egypt.

I sigh deeply trying to find the words to apologize. "I apologize Hussain. I know this is not your fault. You're just the messenger. Tell me, which generals wish to call off the search?"

"Mainly, Kanburni, he says she and her son were probably taken by the harshness of robbers or the desert by now. She is out there alone and poor. How much of a threat can she be?" he says as we talk towards a bench.

As much as I do not want to admit it, he is right. She has no wealth, no supporters in the army, her son was an infant when they ran off in the middle of the night. "Call of the search, but keep a close eye on Kanburni and my 'mother in law.' Can we ever trust people from Walata?" My father could have taken a bride with royal lineage when my mother died, but he wanted the support of the rural people. He plucked a young woman from Walata, a place known for their loose morals.

The next day, father invites Ibn Battuta to tell his stories to the entire royal family under a shaded silk tent while petitioners ask for favors. One by one, dressed in all white, a custom father implemented, subjects ask for loans, blessings to sell their goods, and other favors. Father listens to each one and whispers in my ear as I parrot his decision.

An old woman dressed in white and no shoes shuffles her feet towards us. She bows and opens her mouth, but I command her to stop. I turn to Ibn Batutta. "You have not told of us your time in Walata," I say looking at Aaliyah. He clears his throat and uncomfortably shifts his eyes between Aaliyah and I.

"I found them to be very well read in all things, including The Qur'an," he says brushing the silk pillow bellow him with his hand, refusing eye contact with either of us.

"Mmhmm, what about their social practices? Are the woman chaste?" Aaliyah's face is as still as a wooden tribal mask.

"Both the men and women seem to be...liberal with their marriage vows," he says.

Aaliyah, I must admit is a beauty if I have ever saw one. Her mahogany colored skin and her hair which she refuses to cover. Her

138

hips no doubt is what father was attracted to the most. She has, in all her beauty not yet bore any children, which has drove many in the council mad. I have no children with Rohey out of pure disgust. Father has no son other than me, many see this as the end of the Keita dynasty.

"There are unchaste people everywhere young prince, I am sure Morocco has a fair share too," Aaliyah says glaring at me no doubt speaking of Tida. The fact Rohey is next to me slips my mind as she stands and excuses herself as she walks back to the palace. Ibn Batutta nods his head nervously trying to not offended either of us.

"It seems, Mansa Sulayman has fallen asleep," Ibn Batutta says. The old woman coughs, her knees surely not accustomed to standing so long are beginning to shake. I stand and accept her request without hearing it. I follow Rohey up the steps into the palace. I command her to stop, but she keeps walking. I command her again as se continues to ignore me. I command the guards at the end of the hall to stop her.

I grab her by the arm and take her into the first room I see. "Have you forgotten your place?" I say as she breaks free from my grip.

"Do not forget I did not ask to marry you either," she says. "But I have tried my best to make this work because as much as you hate me, for whatever reason, we are stuck together."

Her nostrils are flaring, making her thin black face seem larger than usual.

"I will not stop seeing Tida," I say. Rohey shakes her head.

"I do not care if you take one hundred wives and one hundred mistresses, you will not embarrass me in public." She narrows her eyes, as if she came to some grand epiphany. "You do know the people hate you? You and your father?"

"Do they hate safe travel roads and trade routes? Do they hate full markets? Do they!" I yell while slowly moving towards her. I once again, grab her by her arm with a tighter grip than before. "Do not forget the Mansa rules with absolute authority and my patiences for you is thin, as is my fathers time in this world."

There is a knock at the door as Tida rises to get dressed. Last night instead of me going to her room she came to mine. A voice from behind the door tells me that Hussain has an important message. I open the door and a letter is handed to me. I run my eyes over each line, then again, the one more time, to make sure I did not misread anything. Tida, no doubt seeing the excitement on my face asks what news I received.

"Aaliyah and Kanburni, they have been caught planning a coup," I say. Tida extends her arm and I hand her the paper. I rush out of the door to find Hussain. When I reach his office he is sitting with a merchant from Asia. I dismiss the merchant and demands more news. Hussain tells me that he did as instructed and has been following Kanburni. He has been recruiting mercenaries from Walata. With this news, I tell Hussain to ready the troops for a march on Walata.

"That will not be necessary, the military was sent there weeks ago," he says sternly.

"I was not consulted?" I ask.

Hussain shakes his head. "You are not Mansa and I was demanded by your father to keep this from you until today. If you notice, there is no commotion in the hallways, there is no scandal. Your father has called for the arrest of Aaliyah and Kanburni, which will happen within the hour."

In total shock I cannot find the words to respond to being left in the dark. "It is vital that nobody knows it was a coup. People must think this was at best a failed assassination by two siblings." I nod my head. "The official story is that Aaliyah and Kanburni tried to poison your father and they failed."

Puzzled and confused I ask Hussain how long has he truly been following them, tracking their moves. "A week before your father sent their family a marriage proposal," Hussain says.

"Samira and her son, did you stop looking for them?" I ask.

"Two bodies were discovered, years ago, a woman and a child. Their wagon was looted. We found a poem on the woman, written by Magha. We suspect Samira tried to flee with a wagon of gold and was robbed on the road to her destination."

This entire time I have simply been playing Mansa. My father has been in control this entire time. Playing the feeble old man role from the beginning.

"Your father wants to speak to you," Hussain says opening the door. I remember as a child, when I would be sent to talk to my father after getting in trouble. Moving through the palace like a sick lion cub, trying to think of ways to avoid punishment. Not much has changed, but the palace now seems a lot lonelier than before.

I enter father's chambers and he is sitting up in bed, looking healthier that I have ever seen him. He points to a spot on the floor, the same spot he would point to when I was child when he had a lecture to give me.

"You will not speak of the coup to anyone." His voice is strong and sturdy as it was when I was a child. "You will return to your wife," he says finally looking at me. "You will make children and secure our families future. I am having Tida sent back to Morocco with Ibn

141

Batutta." He waves his hand and dismiss me, but calls my name forcing me to stop. "One day you will occupy the throne, that day is far from today."

FES, MOROCCO 1353

"You're a man now," mother says to me as I sit reading. The sun dips below the horizon as she sits next to me on the large floor pillow. I close my book and place it next to me, giving her my full attention. "I had to do many things to make sure you survived. You do understand we are still in danger?"

I nod my head slowly. Mother has told me the story of how she fled Gao with two other women who died before I was five. I am well aware I should be siting on the throne as Mansa of Mali. Mother does not allow me to forget. I comfort her by telling her I will never forget my family history. Tears begin to run down her face and I catch them with my thumb, clearing them from her face.

"I had to do many things to survive, well before I had you," mother says smiling. Her smile is not a happy one, but one of relief. One that says she is surprised she made it through. There is a knock at the door. Mother stands, smooths out her gown and glides across the room to open it. Tida and a tall man wearing a turban enter the house. I have not seen Tida since she left. I hug her as she tells me that she missed me.

"Sister," mother says to Tida as they embrace.

"I have missed you too Tida," I say trying to hide my childish joy.

"Let me introduce you to Ibn Battuta. He is an explorer and very well read," Tida says. Ibn Battuta shakes my hand and bows to mother.

"I am Mari-Dajata and this is my mother Samira," I say proudly. Ibn Battuta looks at us with wide eyes. He opens his mouth to speak, but no words pass.

"You mean you are *the* Mari Dajata? Son of Mansa Qasa? Grandson of," he stops. "Grandson of Mansa Musa?" he finally finishes. I nod. "You are Qasa's wife?" he asks mother. She nods. He looks at Tida then back at us. He sighs deeply trying to absorbed this new information.

"I have some explaining to do," mother says as she invites Ibn Battuta to sit. Mother explains how Tida went to Gao specifically to gain favor with Qasa. Mother knew Tida would be able to seduce him. As mother always says, men are predictable. As Tida opened up to Qasa he returned the favor, stories flowed from his mouth without her having to ask.

"He saw me as a harmless toy. Something he could pick up and put down as he pleased and I played along," Tida says. Tida reaches in her bag and hands mother a letter.

"A coup by his wife?" mother says handing me the letter.

"This is our opening. This is our chance!" I say standing up. Blood pulses through my veins.

"Sit down," mother says. "One step at a time. We must be smart about this. We have the advantage of knowing information that we are not supposed to know. More importantly nobody knows we have it."

I nod my head and sit down. Ibn Battuta points to mother and I and in a slow tone asks why we were still alive. It was said that our bodies were found with a poem that was written by my father.

"We placed the bodies and the poem in the wagon. We made it look like a robbery. Nobody who was looking for us knew what we looked like. As long as they found the poem and a child's body they would believe it was us," mother says.

"So all of this; Tida meeting Qasa, the wagon, moving to Fes, all of this was part of your plan?" Ibn Battuta asks. We all nod our head.

"And now Tida is back home, we can plan the next step," I say.

"Which is?" Ibn Battuta asks.

"Sulayman and Qasa have enemies. I have a lot of gold. Raising an army will not be too hard," mother says while playing with a ruby ring on her finger.

66233751R00087

Made in the USA
Middletown, DE
09 March 2018